Florence Marryat

Driven to Bay

Vol. II

Florence Marryat

Driven to Bay
Vol. II

ISBN/EAN: 9783337047764

Printed in Europe, USA, Canada, Australia, Japan

Cover: Foto ©Andreas Hilbeck / pixelio.de

More available books at **www.hansebooks.com**

BY

FLORENCE MARRYAT,

AUTHOR OF

'LOVE'S CONFLICT,' 'MY OWN CHILD,'
'THE MASTER PASSION,' 'SPIDERS OF SOCIETY,'
ETC., ETC.

IN THREE VOLUMES.

VOL. II.

LONDON:

F. V. WHITE & CO.,

31 SOUTHAMPTON STREET, STRAND, W.C.

1887.

EDINBURGH
COLSTON AND COMPANY
PRINTERS

CONTENTS.

DRIVEN TO BAY.

DRIVEN TO BAY.

CHAPTER I.

MAGGIE.

LARGE passenger vessel like the *Pandora*, that makes voyages of two and three months' duration, without stopping on the way, is a hotbed of flirtation. When the first excitement of a 'life on the ocean wave' has toned down, and the novels are exhausted, and everybody knows everybody, then scandal and courtship become the order of

the day. And what glorious oppor-
tunities such a life presents for ripen-
ing friendship into love. As in
a ballroom the young couples frequent
the conservatories, the stairs, the lobbies,
and hall, anywhere where they can talk
and listen unobserved, so on board-ship
they may be found sneaking about the
after part of the poop, the cabin passages, and the lounges in the saloon.
They make appointments on the side
of the quarter-deck in the dog-watch,
or the first night-watch, and there
remain gazing at the moon and the
stars, or in each other's eyes, discussing astronomy, or marine aquaria, or
the Lord knows what, until the young
lady is summarily ordered below. A
chaperon cannot possibly follow her
charge into every corner of a large ship,
for eighty consecutive days. She might
be able to keep a strict eye over her
in a ballroom, but it would be a herculean
task to accomplish the same feat at sea.

And so a lengthened propinquity on board-ship often brings about marriages and scandals that never would have taken place on shore. It is also a great vehicle for gossip. What have the passengers to whom no one makes love to do but scandalise the rest. From the Captain to the Jemmy Ducks, from the noble lord who is travelling in the state-room for his pleasure, to the humble emigrant whose whole property consists of the bundle he carries about with him, all who are unwary enough to tell any tales about themselves, or conspicuous enough to have tales told of them, supply food for discussion over the afternoon cups of tea, and learn with astonishment a few weeks after how much more their companions know of their lives and actions than they do themselves. The *Pandora* had found the north-east trade winds by this time, and making a south-westerly course, was fast diminishing the distance between her and the line.

Though it was the autumn of the year, it might well have been mistaken for the spring, for the birds seemed to be pairing in all directions. Mr Harland and Miss Vansittart were seldom apart. Captain Lovell was paying all the attention in his power to Alice Leyton, whilst Vernon Blythe was eating his heart out for the love of Iris Hetherley, and cursing his fate for being an officer of the ship instead of a passenger. Mr Fowler, the mysterious, flew like a humming-bird from flower to flower, enlivening the married ladies with morsels of scandal, and complimenting the girls on their beauty and their wit. Every one liked him, but no one had succeeded in discovering who he was, or what he was doing on board the *Pandora*. He had a wonderful knack of changing the conversation directly it veered in his own direction, which made it appear impertinent to pursue a curiosity which he so boldly evaded. In the second cabin, Will Farrell had made himself a general favourite, and more than one lone she creature, unattached, tried hard to induce him to take her in tow. But though he was sociable with all, he was only intimate with one, and that one was Maggie Greet. He had formed quite an attachment for this girl. Had he possessed the means he would have transferred her from the steerage to the second cabin, but he promised himself to make up for that, to her, by-and-by. Meanwhile he spent every spare moment by her side, and on deck they were always together. But Maggie would not be persuaded to go on deck until nightfall, and then she wrapped herself up in what appeared an absurd fashion, considering the warmth of the weather.

'What are you afraid of?' asked Farrell of her one evening. 'You couldn't catch cold if you tried, in these latitudes.'

'Toothache,' replied Maggie mendaciously, 'I have it dreadful sometimes at night.'

'That's because you stop in the cabin too much. You stew down there all day, and then when you come on deck, you feel the difference. You should stop in the open air, like the others do, from morning till night.'

'And what would my poor lady do all by herself, whilst I was taking my pleasure on deck?'

'I know you're very good to Miss Douglas, Maggie. It's *that* that first made me feel I should like to have you for a friend. You're a staunch one, I'm sure. But why not persuade her to come, too? She'll kill herself if she mopes in her berth all the voyage. What's the matter with her? Is she sick?'

'No! she isn't sick.'

'Why doesn't she come on deck then?'

'That's *her* business and not yours, Mr Farrell.'

'True ; but I should like to know a little more about you both. Sometimes you call Miss Douglas your "*lady*," and sometimes your "*friend*." Now, I can guess that you have lived together in England as mistress and servant. But why don't you say so?'

'Have you got any more questions to ask me, Mr Farrell?' said Maggie coolly.

They were sitting on the afterdeck together, and it was nearly dark, except for an oil lamp in the forecastle, that threw an occasional light on the girl's face. Maggie was looking very pretty and pleasant that evening. Her dark eyes were bright and merry; her curly hair was blowing about in the sea breeze; over her head she had twisted a shawl of scarlet and green. Her pertness became her roguish face, and Farrell gazed at her admiringly as he answered,—

'You'll provoke me to ask you something that will make you angry, if you look at me in that fashion, Maggie.'

'And what may that be?'

'A kiss?'

'Well, asking and having is two different things, so I advise you to spare your breath to cool your porridge.'

'Now, you wouldn't be so unkind as that, Maggie. But, seriously, can't you understand *why* I want to know more about you. It isn't idle curiosity. It's because—well, it's because we seem to be rowing pretty much in the same boat. We're going to a new country together, where we've got no friends; so why shouldn't we be friends to each other?'

'We *are*, aren't we? anyway, there's no need for *you* to be more friendly than you are, and I don't quite see how you *could* be.'

'*I* do. I would like to be the closest friend you had,—your friend for life, Maggie. Do you understand me?'

'No,' replied Maggie stoutly, 'I don't.'

'Then I'll make it plainer to you. Will you marry me? I want a wife to make a home for me in the new world, and you suit me down to the ground. If you'll say the word, I'll marry you as soon as we touch land. Is it a bargain?'

'Lor', Mr Farrell, are you poking fun at me?'

'Indeed I am in earnest. I was never more so in my life.'

'But you're a gentleman born, and I'm only a servant. It's right you should know the truth now.'

'Well, I'm not a gentleman by birth, Maggie, though I may look like one to you. I was in the position of a gentleman once, but I lost it through my own folly, and I shall never regain it. I got into sore trouble through the rascality of another; and though I wasn't really guilty, appearances were against me, and I had to give up my place, and take to earning my bread by the labour of my hands. So you see we're pretty equal; and a girl that can cook my dinner, and keep my house clean, is just the sort of wife I shall want in my new home.'

'What has become of the fellow as got you into trouble?' asked Maggie, without noticing his last remark.

'Curse him!' exclaimed Farrell vehemently. 'Don't talk of him, Maggie, or I shall forget myself, and where we are. For I'll tell you a secret, my dear. He's on board this very ship!'

'Lor'! and does he know that you're here too?'

'Yes. I hadn't met him for years until I knocked up against him in the shipping-office. He was taken aback at meeting me, I can tell you, and hearing we were to sail in the same vessel. He tried to square me at first, and then he tried to insult me. But I'll have my revenge on him yet. Wait till I meet him on the other side, and we'll stand up, man to man, till one of us drops—'

'Don't talk in that way, Mr Farrell —*don't !*' cried Maggie, as she seized his clenched hand. 'You make my blood run cold. What good will it be to lose your life for a man like that? It won't undo the wrong.'

'You're right there, Maggie. But it drives me mad to know *what he is*, and then to see him carrying on as if he was a lord, and owned the whole vessel. And all the girls fawning on him, and letting him do as he likes with them. Lord, if they only knew his real character!'

'What is his name, Mr Farrell?'

'His right name is Horace Cain, but he's hiding himself under a false one.'

'And what did he do?'

'I can't tell you that, Maggie, because it might leak out, and it involves us both. He's been my ruin in the old country, d—n him! I don't want him to spoil all my chances in the new.'

'Well, then, I'd try and forget it, if I was you, and never speak to him again. That's more sensible than thinking of revenge.'

'I *will* try and forget it—more, I will promise you never to mention it again—if you will be my wife, Maggie.'

Maggie shook her head.

'No, Mr Farrell—*that* I can't never be.

'But why? Don't you like me?'

She did not answer, and he took her hand.

'Don't say *no* in such a hurry, my dear girl. I'll work for you as long as I have a pair of hands, and I'll make you as happy as I can; and it'll be much more comfortable to come to a home of your own than to serve in that of a stranger. Just think, now. I really like you very much—in fact, I love you, or I wouldn't propose such a thing. Am I disagreeable to you, or can't you love me a little in return?'

But all the answer Maggie gave was conveyed by her throwing her shawl over her face and bursting into a storm of tears.

'Why! what is this? Have I said anything to vex you? Oh, don't, *don't* cry so!' exclaimed Farrell anxiously.

But Maggie sobbed on for a few minutes without intermission. Then, suddenly stopping, she uncovered her face again, and turned to confront him.

'Look here, Mr Farrell,' she said, 'don't you never talk to me about marriage again. I ain't a marrying woman. I shall never marry you, nor no one. Do you understand? I shall remain as I am to the last day of my life.'

'But why? Are you married already?'

The girl laughed harshly.

'No! I ain't, nor likely to be. There's no other man in the way. You needn't fear that.'

'Then I shall go on asking you till you say yes.'

'Mr Farrell! I tell you 'tain't no use. I ain't fit to be your wife. I ain't a good girl. Now, you've got it, straight from the shoulder, and I hope you like it.'

For a moment Farrell was silent. It wasn't a pleasant piece of news to hear, as he interpreted it. But he loved the woman sincerely, and he wouldn't give her up just yet.

'No one is good. I daresay you're no worse than others,' he answered presently.

'Yes I am,' said Maggie, 'I'm downright bad.'

'What do you call "downright bad?"'

'I don't know why I should tell you,' whimpered Maggie, wiping away a fresh relay of tears; 'but you've been very kind and good to me and my dear mistress, and I wouldn't like you to think that I'm ungrateful. And I'm sure you won't tell on me.'

'God forbid!' exclaimed Farrell solemnly.

'Well, then, I had a misfortune, and I went wrong,' whispered Maggie, in a very low voice.

'Poor child! Was it long ago?'

'Better than two years. I was only seventeen.'

'And where's the brute that wronged you?' exclaimed Farrell fiercely.

'Hush,' cried Maggie, looking round her nervously. 'Don't speak so loud. It's all over now. It *has* been ever since. I thought him good and true at that time, but when I found out what a villain he was (and much worse to others than he'd been to me), my love turned to hate, and I could have killed him— except for others.'

'And who are the others?'

'I can't tell you. 'Tisn't my secret. It's theirs. But you know all now. And that's the reason I can't be your wife. You wouldn't have asked me if you'd known.'

'Does Miss Douglas know your secret, Maggie?'

'No, no,' cried the girl excitedly, 'and don't you never hint it to her, or I'll kill you. Oh, my dear, sweet mistress! I've tried sometimes to make her understand, but I haven't dared tell her the truth. I should die if I saw her sweet eyes look angry at me. Oh, promise me, Mr Farrell, on your sacred honour, that you'll never let her guess I've been so wicked. For I'm her only comfort. There's no one else to love and care for her, and if she made me leave her, she'd be all alone. And she's in such dreadful trouble you can't think. If it's wrong to stay by her—so pure and good as she is — I can't help it, for I'd lay down my life for her sake.'

She turned her face, all blurred and swollen with her tears, towards him, as she spoke, and he bent down and kissed it tenderly.

'Poor child! I will carry your secret for ever in the depths of my heart. And

now, answer my question—Will you be
my wife ? '

' Lor' ! Mr Farrell, you can't have
listened to a word I said.'

' I heard you perfectly, and I understand
you have been wronged and betrayed by
a villain. So have I ! and I am the worst
of the two. We have each yielded to
the temptation that assailed us. We are
equally guilty, and I believe equally peni-
tent. We have no right to reproach each
other. If your past is as entirely buried
as mine, Maggie, let us try to console
each other in the future.'

' Oh, sir ! you are too good to me ! I
don't deserve it. I didn't think any honest
man would ever think of me now.'

' You must call me " *Will*," Maggie.'

' When I'm accustomed to the idea a
bit, I may. But I can't believe it's
true.'

' It rests with you to make it so.'

' *To be your wife !* ' said Maggie
musingly—' to be your lawful, married

wife, and have a home of my own in New Zealand. Oh, Mr Farrell,' she continued suddenly, as the conviction burst upon her, ' I shall never *never* forget your goodness to the last hour of my life, and I'll be as true as steel to you, if only in gratitude for what you've said to-day.'

CHAPTER II.

IN THE DOLDRUMS.

IDED by the steady trades, the *Pandora* crept up to the line, and in little more than a month from her date of sailing she crossed that invisible goal, and fell in with a dead calm in the horse latitudes.

It was a changeable day, but close and sultry, and the heat between decks was intolerable. The sun occasionally peeped out from behind black clouds, and cast his scorching rays upon the troubled waters, which rose and fell in angry chops, like the breast of an indignant woman.

Everything was done to conciliate the fickle wind, but without avail. It behaved like a spoilt child, which is never happy unless acting in a contrary direction to what others desire. The yards were squared in, as it hauled aft, but before the ropes were coiled up the provoking element was round on the other quarter, and the shellbacks manned the forebrace. Then it went right ahead, and the unfortunate officer of the watch was compelled to box his yard, and have the trouble of getting the *Pandora* on her course again in a dead calm. Heavy squalls came up from all points of the compass, and while they passed over the vessel sent her galloping along at a splendid pace. But in half-an-hour their force would expend itself; and torrents of rain poured down and left the ship again in the doldrums. The officers were weary of slacking away braces and countermanding orders; the sailors' hard hands, soaked with the rain, became sore and chafed; and the passengers were grumbling and discontented, because they were unable to remain on deck.

The 'boatswains,' with their snowy plumage and long spiked-tail feathers, sailed overhead, uttering shrill cries to their mates, but not attempting to pounce down upon the flying fish which swam in shoals close to the surface of the water, and the 'shipjacks' and 'bonitas' rose frequently into the air, and fell lazily back upon the billows with an awkward splash. Even the merry little 'Mother Carey's chickens' had ceased their continuous flight, and come to an anchor in the wake of the vessel, where they rode up and down on the blue, mountainous waves.

Yet the rain was refreshing. It was not a cold pitiless storm, nor a searching Scotch mist, but fell in a regular tropical downpour — a drenching volume of warm water, that splashed in huge drops upon the decks, that ran down the masts and rigging in a delightful shower-bath, that washed the salt spray from the boats and spars, and made the ship clean and fresh. Had these frequent squalls not mitigated the fierceness of the sun's rays, the decks would have been unbearable, the sailors would have been obliged to adopt shoe leather, and the pitch would have boiled out of the seams, and stuck to everything with which it came in contact. But under the influence of the rain the shellbacks pattered about with bare feet, enjoying the cool bath, and not even taking the trouble to don their oilskins to protect them from a wetting. Few people on shore know the true character of our English sailors — fewer still have ever tried to find out what sort of animals they are. There is a general opinion held by the land-lubber that the sailor is a rollicking, devil-me-care, blasphemous creature, with a wife in every port,—a great capacity for rum, and a tendency to sing, ' Yeo heave, oh' upon every possible occasion. But the real seaman is very different from this. There is no such man as the brainless fool who is depicted in drawing-room songs and on the stage as constantly 'hoisting up his slacks' and 'tipping his flippers,' and singing out ' Hillee Haulee,' or some equally childish refrain.

The British sailor is certainly partial to rum, and he has every reason to be so. When on a freezing night he is perched for a couple of hours on the footrope of a yard, trying to handle an obstinate top-sail, which has torn the nails from his fingers, and caused him to tuck his chin down to his breast to head against the biting wind ; when this uninviting task is completed, a lot of strong rum goes down like mother's milk, warming the very cockles of his heart, and giving him fresh vigour and endurance to battle with the storm.

Then with regard to the fairer sex, a sailor's gallantry is a byword, and what more natural than it should be so. It is so seldom he can enjoy female society, and after having been located for months in a forecastle, and subjected to the rough horse-play of his male companions, the ways and words of women (even though they may be the lowest of their sex) is a welcome change, and acts on the susceptible nature of Jack like a charm. He adores woman collectively and individually. At sea he sings her praises, and he boasts of her virtues in every clime. He swears eternal fidelity to her before he leaves England, and breaks his promise at the first port he touches at—still *woman*, as a noun of multitude, is responsible for it all. And when he returns home, he is as enthusiastic over Poll as if he had never forgotten her for a single minute. His creed may be summed up in the refrain of the ballad—

> ' It don't matter what you do,
> So long as the heart's true,
> And his heart *is* true to Poll.'

But the British seaman has sterling qualities to counterbalance the frivolity of his child-like nature. To stand by his shipmates in times of trouble or sickness—to evince a strong attachment to little children—to be honest and above-board in his dealings—to defend the weak and punish the bully — to remember kind actions and forget petty injustices, these are some of the virtues which stand out boldly in the characters of our sailors, and more than counterbalance any little failings of which they may be guilty. They are rough and straightforward, preferring to settle an argument by the use of their fists, than by philosophical reasoning. They are brave and fearless,—careless of death, though they live under the daily chance of becoming acquainted with Davy Jones' locker, and yet simple in their faith as little children.

The sailors before the mast of the *Pandora* were sixteen in number—twelve able-bodied seamen and four ordinaries, who were all comfortably housed in the forecastle, which was certified to accommodate twenty-four hands. Their work at times, when the ship required box-hauling and tacking, was not light, as the *Pandora* was heavily rigged, and only carried part of her complement. They were not all English, amongst them being Swedes, Germans, and Spaniards, who dressed in blue and red 'jumpers,' and made a picturesque group when at work together. There is always one officer who is singled out as a favourite by the seamen, and on the *Pandora* a unanimous verdict was passed in favour of Vernon Blythe. The chief mate was gruff and tyrannical, and his orders were frequently accompanied by unnecessary oaths, which lowered him in their estimation. The third officer was only a newly-fledged mate, who had just hopped from the midshipman's berth, and, though holding a certificate, was looked on by the sailors as a mere boy, and treated consequently with a respectful but patronising interest. The 'old man,' as they designated their skipper, was not disliked, though by no means a favourite. When at the wheel, or in the captain's quarters, he never interfered with them, but his indefatigable system of working up was not appreciated.

For a whole fortnight the *Pandora* was making but little headway in the doldrums, and during that period the sailors were continually working ship. The captain raised the clews of his courses, and lowered them again; ran up the head sails, and then manned the downhauls; set the spanker, and trailed it in again. Everything was done by turn to work the vessel out of those detestable latitudes, and he did not spare his crew, which aggravated them to such an extent, that they growled from morning till night, and rained imprecations on their commander's head, which, if put into effect, would have enriched the coffers of his satanic majesty.

Early one morning a treacherous squall burst upon the *Pandora*, which threw

her for a few seconds on her beam ends,
till she was righted by the cool pluck of
Mr Coffin, who ordered the halliards to
be let go ; and perceiving the yards
would not come down, took charge of
the helm himself, and shivered the weather
leeches, which righted the ship, though
she sailed within an inch of being taken
flat aback, and losing her sticks.   When
she was out of danger, Captain Robarts
considered it necessary to stay the vessel,
as she was many points out of her course,
and the order was given to ''bout ship.'
The decks were now dry, and the breeze
fresh and invigorating.   The passengers
had crowded on the knife-board to see
the *Pandora* '*turned round*'—an operation
which was new to them.   The ropes were
cleared for running, and the hands stationed ; and when clean full ' Sea-oh ! '
was passed to the chief mate, who, with
a few men, was standing by to ease off
the jib sheets on the topgallant forecastle.
When within a point and a half of the

wind, and the sails were hugging the masts, the order was shouted to 'crossjack haul,' and the hands of the main fife-rail gathered in the slack of the braces, which whizzed and cracked through the blocks at the opposite side, as the heavy yards swung round.

But when square the lower yard brought up with a sudden jerk, and refused to be pointed.

'What's foul?' roared Captain Robarts.

'There's something in the starboard crossjack braceblock, sir,' replied the third officer.

'Send a hand up to clear it, then,' bawled the irate skipper.

Now it happened that the ship's washerwoman had taken advantage of the recent rainy weather to collect a quantity of fresh water, and that very morning had hung her clean linen to dry on a small line suspended over the deck, between the main shrouds. The velocity of the braces as they ran up aloft

made them twist and curl and assume
fantastic shapes, and as they careered in
close proximity to the wet clothing, a
mysterious garment was caught up, and
became jammed in the block.   One of
the sailors ran up the ratlines, and clambered into the top; and, by a strong pull
from below, the garment was disengaged.
The language of the officers was high
Dutch to the passengers assembled on
the poop, but from the visible excitement
of the captain, they guessed that something must have gone wrong, and watched
the seaman curiously, as he hastened up
the rope ladder.

'What is it?' shouted the skipper, as he
saw the block was cleared.

The sailor in the maintop did not
answer, but glanced slyly down at his shipmates, and then at the red flannel garment
he held in his hand; whilst the ladies and
gentlemen stood in a group together, and
looked on with breathless interest.

'It is something *red*!' exclaimed Alice

Leyton, who was very close to Captain
Lovell. 'What on earth can it be? Is it
a flag, Jack?' she asked of Vernon, who
stood just below them.

'I don't know, Alice, but I don't think
it is,' replied Jack, who seemed unaccountably amused.

'It is just the colour of baby's new
pinafores. I shall be sorry if one of them
gets torn,' said Mrs Leyton.

'What is it?' repeated the captain, in
a louder voice. 'D—n it! Hold it out,
man.'

Without hesitation the sailor obeyed.
He held the mysterious obstacle out at
arm's length, and the breeze, catching it
on the right quarter, unfurled it like a flag,
and it remained distended in the air for
the benefit of all beholders. It was made
of red flannel—it appeared to be divided
into two parts like twin bolster-covers on
one stalk—and it looked as if it would fit
Mrs Vansittart.

The silence which followed its appear-

ance lasted for a minute only. Then the
ladies blushed crimson, and with subdued
exclamations of horror hid their faces
behind their fans or in the pages of their
novels. The gentlemen, with ill-concealed
smiles, turned away, lest their amusement
should confuse still further their fair companions ; and the boisterous sailors with
one accord burst into loud shouts of laughter, which, for the moment, was beyond
the power of their officers to control.

The grim and pious captain even was
moved by the liberal display of that
sacred, though unmentionable article of
female clothing, and was obliged to bite his
lip and stamp his feet lest his noisy crew
should take advantage of his loss of self-
command. Then assuming his usual dig-
nified manner, he bellowed out an order
in a deep, stern voice, that made every
sailor hasten to the forebraces, and for a
time forget the comical little adventure
which had upset the order and equanimity
of the *Pandora.*

Vernon Blythe walked away to the lower deck with a broad smile upon his face. He had laughed as heartily as the rest, until a distressed look from Alice Leyton had recalled him to a sense of duty. But now, as he found himself alone, the comical appearance of the red flannel bolster cases, as they inflated in the breeze, came back forcibly upon his mind, and he laughed out loud. How closely connected are joy and sorrow, comedy and tragedy, in this world. Vernon was striding along, with a beaming smile upon his handsome features, and his eyes lit up with merriment, when he came suddenly upon *Iris Harland.* He had longed and prayed to see her again ; he had tried every manœuvre he could think of to come upon her unawares, but without success, and he had almost begun to think there was no chance for him. And yet now, when he was least expecting it, here she was in the second cabin, seated at the end of the table, with her head bent wearily upon her hand. In a moment the light had faded from Jack's face, to give place to a look of anxious expectation. But he did not hesitate. His chance was come, and he would take it. He walked straight up to her side.

CHAPTER III.

THE WIDOW.

'MISS HETHERLEY!' he ex-
claimed, in a voice that trembled with nervousness and excitement. 'Miss Hetherley, will you not
speak to me?'

Iris was not unprepared for the meeting, although a moment before she had
believed herself to be alone. She had
talked the matter over with Maggie, and
they had agreed that it was impossible
she could avoid him for the whole course
of the voyage, and that, sooner or later,
Vernon Blythe and she must speak to one

another again. Yet what to say to him, or how to explain her presence on board the *Pandora*, she knew not, and her first refuge was in an attempt at denial.

'I am not Miss Hetherley,' she answered, in a low voice, and with her face turned from him.

'Forgive me. I know you are married, but I never heard the name of your husband. How am I to address you?'

'You — you — are mistaken,' repeated Iris. 'I am *Miss Douglas.*'

Vernon looked down at her for a few moments in silence, his young, lithe figure drawn up to its full height, as he stood beside her. She—still drooping over the table, hid her burning face as best she could from him.

'Iris,' he said presently, 'why do you want to deceive me?'

At that appeal—so tenderly spoken— she broke down, and began to cry.

'Oh, don't do *that*, for Heaven's sake!' exclaimed Vernon. 'If you wish to avoid

me—if my presence is obnoxious to you
—say so, and I will go away, and never
come near you again. But don't cry. It
is more than I can stand. If you are
in trouble, let me help you. Am I not
your friend ?'

' I have no friends,' sobbed Iris.

' *No friends!'* he echoed reproachfully.
' Have you then quite forgotten Dunmow,
and the Bridge of Allan ?'

Forgotten them. How she wished that
she could forget them. As Vernon spoke,
a vision rose before her of the heather-
covered hills, the rippling burns, the blue,
misty sky of far-off Scotland, where she
had first met him, and, above them all,
the earnest, pleading, passionate young
face that had implored her to exchange
her heart for his. How often she had
thought of it since. How often had the
memory of his eyes, swimming in a mist
of unshed tears, come between her and
the disappointment of her married life.
How often, when the scales had fallen

from her own vision, and the man she
had believed to be a god had proved to
be the commonest of clay, had Iris Harland not wished she had been a little less
hasty, and taken time to weigh the several
merits of the men who had asked to link
their lot with hers.   And as Vernon's soft
voice, sounding so different when he
spoke to her from what it did when he
spoke to others, fell on her ear, it brought
the past so vividly before her, she could
not stay her tears.

'Have you quite forgotten?' he repeated. 'When you crushed the best hope
of my life, Iris, you left me one consolation—you promised to remain my friend.
But that promise is still unredeemed.   I
heard that you were married, but nothing
more.   I have never forgotten you, but I
had no hope we should meet again.   Now
that it has happened so unexpectedly, I
find you alone — in trouble — and in a
position utterly unfitted for you.   Won't
you fulfil your old promise now?   Won't

you let me be your friend, and help you as far as lies in my power? Where is your husband?'

'I have no husband,' she answered, blushing furiously.

'No husband!' cried Vernon. 'Was it a mistake then? Have you never been married?'

Iris nodded her head.

'And he is dead?'

The girl started. She had never thought of this solution to the difficulty. Of course she would pass herself off as a widow. Nothing could be easier. The anxious expression in a great measure left her face as it occurred to her. She did not foresee the dilemma it might create for them both.

'Yes,' she answered, almost eagerly, 'he is dead. I am alone.'

'And your father. Is he gone too?'

'Yes, thank God. I mean that it would have broken his heart to see the trouble I have gone through.'

'Then you have known trouble, poor child, as well as I ? '

'Yes,' she said, shivering; 'plenty! Please don't speak of it.'

'And why are you going out to New Zealand ?   Have   you   friends   there ? What do you expect to do ? '

'I don't know.'

'But, good heavens ! you cannot land in a strange country without a protector, or a home to go to—without any plans, or visible means of subsistence. Miss Hetherley, forgive me, but—'

'Pray—*pray* don't call me by that name,' she interposed fearfully. 'You don't know—there might be people on board—you never can tell.'

'Miss Douglas, then ; but how can I address you by a name that is not yours? I shall be constantly forgetting. Let me call you *Iris*. I would not be presumptuous, but I have thought and dreamt of you by that name ever since we parted. May I call you so now ? '

'As you will, Mr Blythe.'

'Then, Iris, tell me all your troubles.'

'Oh, I cannot!' she said, shrinking backward. 'You do not know.'

'But I cannot help guessing. I guess, from finding you here, that you are not rich. I guess, from the few words you have uttered, that you are lonely and unhappy. I can see for myself that you are ill. Iris! can I be your friend and stand by in silence and make no effort to help you? Let me speak to you openly once more. It is five years since we parted, but not a feeling of my heart has changed since then. Cannot you trust me to be true and faithful to your interests now? I have had very little consolation during those five years. You denied me the greatest happiness of my life, and I submitted to your decree. But you can in a measure console me now. Confide your troubles to me, and let me help to bear them with you. How long have you been a widow?'

'Oh, a long time! I never really had a husband. I was widowed from the commencement.'

'Poor child! I couldn't have turned out a worse "spec." myself. And where have you been living since?'

'In London!'

'Why did you leave it?'

'Oh, Mr Blythe, don't ask me so many questions! It is the fear of your doing so that has made me avoid you hitherto. If we are to be friends, learn to spare me. I *cannot* speak of the past.'

'Will you speak of the future, then?'

'Yes! when the time comes, perhaps. But it is no use discussing it in the present. It may never come to pass. We may not reach land. I wish to God I were not to do so! I would like to throw myself overboard at once, and make an end to all things.'

Vernon Blythe looked very grave. This expression of despair on the part of the woman he would have died to save, cut him to the quick. There sat his ideal,—the creature who had spoiled the best part of his life,—whom he had dreamed of, longed for, and yearned after for five long years out of five-and-twenty. There she sat, side by side with him again—free—friendless—almost, as it were, at his mercy—and yet he felt as far from her as ever. As those last passionate words burst from Iris's lips, he rose to his feet.

'I am worrying you,' he said gently; 'I won't stay here any longer. But whatever may be your trouble, Iris, whether it arises from loss, or poverty, or—or — anything else — don't be afraid to ask my assistance or advice. Remember, I am your friend : and I have the best right of all men to be so, because I—'

But here he stopped short, fearful of offending her, and the conscious blood dyed his fair face crimson.

'What were you going to say?' demanded Iris presently.

'What perhaps I had better leave un-
said.   But you are a woman, and do
not need words to make you understand.
You have but to think of the Bridge of
Allan, to know *why* I have good right to
be your friend.'

'You will not speak of me to—to any
one else on board?' she said anxiously,
as she laid her hand upon his arm.

Vernon looked down at the fair white
hand lying so lightly on the blue sleeve
of his uniform, and trembled with pleas-
urable excitement.   How he longed to
raise it to his lips.   But he resisted the
temptation.

'Of course not.   Do you think I go
about making my most sacred feelings
public property?   Your name has never
passed my lips to a soul since the day
we parted.'

'Did you care for me like *that?*' said
Iris, opening her lovely hazel eyes.

'I cared for you—*like my soul!*' he answered, in a low voice.

There was silence between them for a few minutes after that, and then he resumed, in a lighter tone,—

'Why do you seclude yourself so much in this dark cabin? No wonder you look pale and drooping,—like a broken flower. You should come more on deck. I have looked for you again and again there in vain. I thought you were determined not to speak to me during the whole voyage.'

'I am afraid—' commenced Iris nervously.

'Afraid of what?'

'Oh, I don't know. Some one on board might recognise me—and I would rather not. I don't wish any one to know.'

'Have you seen the list of passengers?'

'Yes,' she said, with a shudder.

The young officer noticed the shudder.

'Well, then, come on the quarter-deck at night, and no one will see you, especially if you put on a veil. But do come! You will be ill if you remain here. And then when it is not my watch I shall be able to sit by you and talk to you and cheer you up. Will you promise to come?'

'Yes. I will go with Maggie to-night, if I am well enough.'

'And I will leave you now, because you have had enough of me, and the passengers are coming down to their dinner.'

He took her slender hand within his own.

'God bless you, Iris! Remember, you are not friendless any longer.'

For the first time, then, she raised her eyes and looked well at him. His were regarding her steadfastly. Over his manly features a great veil of tenderness seemed to have drawn itself, and his sensitive mouth was quivering with emotion. He was looking at her as we gaze at a wounded animal, or a dying infant, with

infinite compassion, and a strong desire
to relieve and protect. And at that
moment, how Iris longed for his protection.

'Oh, you are *good!*' she cried suddenly. ' I am not afraid of you. I will
trust you, and some day I will tell you
all!'

'You have made me happier than I
can say,' replied Vernon, as he laid a
reverent kiss upon her hand, and turned
away.

As he found himself on deck again,
he could have sung aloud for joy. The
desire of his heart was accomplished!
He had found her again — she would
allow him to befriend her—above all, she
was *free!* This secret love of his life,
whom he had believed lost to him for
ever, was actually by his side, and at
liberty to be wooed, and perhaps won!

His pulses galloped as he thought of
it. His brain whirled. He was capable
of committing any extravagance. His

mind ran riot, and sped away to the time when he should again tell Iris that he loved her, and hear her lips confess that he had won her at last. Oh! if the chance ever presented itself, he would never, *never* let her go until she had promised to reward his patient love by becoming his wife.

And just as he thought this, and sprang up the companion, he came face to face with Alice Leyton!

'Hullo, Jack!' she exclaimed, 'what have you been doing to yourself? Your face is as red as a turkey cock!'

'I think I might return the compliment,' he said, as he watched her blushing cheeks. 'But I can't stay, Alice, I have some duty to attend to.'

'You *must* stay!' cried the young lady imperiously. 'I have something to say to you. I've been making love to the captain—*awful* love. Now, don't get jealous, Jack.'

'If I did *that* every time you flirted

with another fellow, Alice, I might play Blue Beard all day long,' remarked her lover.

'But this was absolutely necessary— I was martyred in a good cause,' resumed Miss Leyton. 'I wanted to get his leave for us to have private theatricals on board, and the dear old thing has given it without a demur.'

'You *have* worked wonders then. We have always considered the skipper too pious to countenance any such frivolity.'

'Well, he wasn't too pious with me, I can tell you ; and he has promised to come and see me act into the bargain.'

'So you are coming out as a leading lady, eh, Alice ? '

'Of course; you didn't suppose I should take all that trouble for somebody else, did you ? Miss Vere says she will help us. I and Captain Lovell, and Miss Vansittart and Mr Harland, will all take

a part. And *you* too. You will play my
lover, won't you, Jack?'

'No, Alice, I think not, thank you.
You have so many lovers, real and
imaginary, that one more or less can
make no difference; and private theatricals are not in my line.'

'Oh, you disagreeable old thing! It's
most horrid of you to leave me to be
made love to by a lot of strange gentlemen. They'll have to kiss me, remember, if it's in the piece.'

'You won't let them, unless you like
it; I am sure of that,' replied Jack,
swinging himself on to the poop, and
proceeding on his way.

'You're a wretch!' called out Alice
after him, but he only laughed in return;
yet his spirits had suddenly gone down
to zero. What had he been thinking of
and dreaming of when he encountered
her? What a fool he was to forget for
a moment that he was bound to Alice
Leyton, and could not in honour marry

any other woman. Of what folly had he not been guilty? His heart sank under the conviction, but he pulled himself together like a man, and tried hard to stamp down his disappointment. After all, he could be Iris's friend. She had said so with her own sweet lips, and her faithful friend he was determined to prove, until death came to separate them.

CHAPTER IV.

ON THE POOP DECK.

O one on board the *Pandora* was a greater favourite than Alice Leyton. She was pretty and lively and clever, and she was reported to be rich. On first starting, she had confided the secret of her engagement to Vernon Blythe to several of the lady passengers, and, as is usual in such cases, the news had leaked out, until it was the property of the whole vessel. When she found that it was so, Alice became shy of its being alluded to, and on more than one occasion had denied it point blank, so that people did not really know what

to believe about it. And the girl had
not been in such good spirits lately. She
laughed and talked enough when on
deck or in the saloon, and she 'chaffed'
Jack Blythe so unmercifully whenever
they met, that he had become rather
weary of her presence. But when she
found herself alone or unobserved, Alice's
face told a very different tale. Even the
baby, little Winnie, who shared her cabin,
had more than once been wakened from
sleep by her sister's sobbing, and wondered in her childish way if 'Ally's
pain was very bad,' to make her 'cry so
hard?' Indeed Alice Leyton's conduct at
this period resembled nothing so much
as an April day, with its alternate sun
and showers. Her tears might flow fast
at night, but she would appear on deck
next morning, radiant with smiles, and
her mother was the only person who
noticed that she looked a little care-
worn, and that the lines under her blue
eyes were a shade darker than was

natural.   Mrs Leyton noticed another
thing—that her daughter no longer made
the strenuous efforts she used to do to
secure a *tête-à-tête* with her lover, Jack
Blythe, but seemed quite contented with
the somewhat formal greetings they were
obliged to exchange in public, whilst she
spent hour after hour in the company of
Captain Lovell.   But she did not mention
the subject to Alice.   She preferred the
girl should settle her love affairs in her
own way.   The truth is, Mrs Leyton
had never felt quite easy as to what her
husband would say when she told him
she had allowed their eldest daughter to
consider herself engaged to be married
before consulting him.   She was a great
invalid herself.   She had come to England before Winnie's birth to secure better
medical advice than she was able to get
in New Zealand, and it had not been
considered safe for her to return home
until now.   Alice had been, therefore, from
the age of fourteen to eighteen, under

her mother's exclusive care, and Mrs
Leyton often wished she had not allowed
her to drift into this quasi-engagement
with Vernon Blythe. Her husband was
a wealthy man, the owner of a large
sheep - run on the Hurannie, and was
likely to expect his daughters to contract
marriages in accordance with the settle-
ments he was able to make upon them.
Mrs Leyton felt sure that of the two
suitors for Alice's hand, her husband
would prefer Captain Lovell, who had
retired from the service, and was going out
to settle in New Zealand, and so she
determined to let matters take their course.
She liked and admired Vernon Blythe,
but he had no money beyond his pay,
and nothing but his good looks and
gentlemanly manners to recommend him
for a husband. Alice, on the other
hand, was in a very unhappy frame of
mind. She wished her mother would
broach the subject, and ask for her confidence, or that Jack would grow jealous

of her flirtation with Lovell, and so bring about an explanation, but neither of them made any sign. She felt guiltily happy in the presence of the fascinating captain, and basely false and fickle with regard to Jack ; and if he held her to her engagement, she felt that she must marry him, and so she was miserable all round. For she knew now that she had never really loved Vernon Blythe. It was a folly—an infatuation. He was so handsome, so graceful,—so courteous in his manners towards her, and all the sex. But he had never looked at her as Captain Lovell looked. She had never heard his voice tremble while he addressed her, nor lowered to such a whisper that no one but herself could understand what he said. Jack was the first man who had ever made her heart beat a little quicker. He had always been lively and *debonnair* with her, and paid her compliments and brought her such trifles as his slender purse could afford, and she had mistaken her girlish pleasure over a sentimental friendship as an indication of the master passion.

But poor Alice knew the difference now, and the knowledge made her miserable, as it does most of us.

The *Pandora*, with the aid of the trades, was still forging ahead, but day by day as she approached the Antarctic latitudes, it was growing colder, and the Southern Cross was plainly visible at night. Yet the hours passed but slowly, and had it not been for the anticipated private theatricals, the passengers would have had but little to talk about.

They were all assembled one morning on the poop. Alice and Captain Lovell were standing close together, talking to Miss Vere about their proposed amusement, and the conversation naturally led on to the subject of her profession.

'By Jove! deucedly jolly, Miss Vere, you know, to be on the stage; isn't it now, eh?' lisped Harold Greenwood, who was once more in the full glory of pink ties and white waistcoats, and had his glass well screwed into his eye.

'Have you tried it, Mr Greenwood ?'

'Well, not exactly, you know. But I might have, if I had chosen. I was offered a large salary once—a *tremendous* salary, I was told it was—to appear as " Romeo." The manager said I was just the face and figure for " Romeo," you know. " Oh that I wath a glove upon that cheek," and all that sort of thing, eh ? I'd like doosidly to play " Romeo" to your " Juliet," Miss Vere, do you know ? You *have* played " Juliet," haven't you, eh ?'

' Sometimes,' replied the actress quietly.

' Oh, I am *sure* you have. You'd be an ideal Juliet, you know. I fancy I can hear you saying to me, " Oh, Womeo, Womeo ! wherefore art thou, Womeo ?" ' exclaimed Mr Greenwood, lisping rather worse than usual, in his excitement. But he was quite offended when every one joined in a loud laugh.

'Oh, you must excuse us, really, Mr Greenwood !' exclaimed Miss Vere, wiping her eyes, 'but you *are* so funny. I should like to play " Juliet " with you excessively. I assure you I should.'

'*Do*, then,' cried Harold Greenwood, taking it all in earnest ; 'let us have " Romeo and Juliet " instead of this stupid comedy, and I shall have the bliss (if for only one night) of pwetending you are mine, don't you know ?'

'I am afraid it would take too much of our time,' replied Miss Vere, with mock seriousness. 'You do not know the many years of hard study that I was obliged to go through, before I dared attempt the part of Juliet.'

'But I thought you had only been for a few years on the stage,' remarked Captain Lovell.

'Oh, no ! indeed you are mistaken. For the last five years I have been on the London boards, but I struggled for thirteen years in the provinces before

I could command an appearance in town.'

'Do you mean to say you have been eighteen years on the stage, Miss Vere?' said Alice incredulously. 'You must have appeared when you were very young.'

'I was ten years old when I made my *début*. My father was an actor at the Grecian Theatre, and as soon as I was old enough to speak my lines correctly, he procured me my first engagement in the pantomime of "Goody Two Shoes."'

'By Jove! I should like to play in a pantomime, Miss Vere, don't you know?' drawled Harold Greenwood; 'it must be very jolly to make-believe to be a cat, or a dog, eh?'

'Or a monkey, Mr Greenwood. No, I don't think you would care about it. You would soon want to cancel your engagement. It is all noise and nonsense and make-up.'

'Mr Greenwood is so clever, I don't think he would have much trouble to make-up—as a monkey,' remarked Captain Lovell dryly.

Miss Vere frowned, and bit her lip.

'A pantomime is all very nice from the front,' she continued ; 'but when you are obliged to listen to the same music night after night, to hear the same lines spoken, the same "gags" used, you soon get sick and tired of it all. However, I owe so much to my burlesque training, that I never regret I went through it.'

'But how could it do *you* any good?' demanded Alice Leyton.

'It taught me to use my arms and legs, my dear, and cured me of many bad habits, such as not being able to stand still, or to speak distinctly. There are very few of our best-known artists who have not played in pantomime or burlesque, and some of our leading ladies have commenced their career in the ballet.'

'But there are many actresses who play leading parts all at once, don't you know,' said Harold Greenwood. 'I know a young lady who acted " Juliet " on her first appearance, at a *matinée*. What do you say to that, Miss Vere, eh ? '

' I say she may have *attempted* the part, but I am quite sure she never *acted* it as it should be done. " Juliet " is at once the most beautiful and most difficult of Shakespeare's creations, and in the hands of a novice it becomes a burlesque.'

' But she had heaps of bouquets, you know,' argued Mr Greenwood : ' the stage was quite covered with them.'

' Flowers do not denote a success now-a-days,' replied Miss Vere, ' and to an amateur they become a very empty compliment. If your lady friend wished to gratify her vanity, and prove how well she looked in antique dresses, she might have found a less ridiculous and expensive way of doing it. You may think I am a little hard, perhaps,' she added, ' but I confess I *am* severe on those amateurs, who have done so much towards lowering the

prestige of one of the most noble profes-
sions in the world.'

'Oh, Miss Vere, you make us feel so
small!' cried Alice. 'I shall never dare
attempt the part of " Julia," after what you
have said.'

' My dear girl, what nonsense! My
remarks were never meant to apply to
our projected amusement. You will certainly take " Julia," and make a very
charming " Julia " into the bargain ; and I
am sure Captain Lovell will make a
" Faulkner " to match.

The captain bowed.

' If I could only have been the lover of
" Lydia Languish,"' he said.

' Go along, you humbug!' cried the
actress merrily ; 'you know that " Faulkner" will become twice as natural an
impersonation in your hands. Indeed,
I think you will have to moderate your
dramatic ardour a little, or we shall have a
certain young gentleman in uniform interrupting the rehearsals—eh, Miss Leyton?'

'I don't know what you're alluding to,' said Alice, with a vivid blush.

'It must be something to do with the temperature of these latitudes,' observed Miss Vere meaningly, 'but I observe that the further south we go, the harder Miss Leyton finds it to understand any of my hints.'

'Now you are growing abusive, so I shall run away,' replied Alice merrily, as she turned to the after part of the vessel.

Captain Lovell raised his hat to Miss Vere, and followed her.

'Oh! are *you* here?' she said, with well-affected surprise, as having ensconced herself by the wheel-house, she found the captain seated by her side.

'Yes! Am I intruding?' demanded Lovell.

'Oh, no! of course not; besides, the wheel-house does not belong to me. Only I wish—' said the girl, looking down—'I *do* wish people wouldn't be disagreeable, and talk so.'

'I wouldn't mind their talking, if it

wasn't true,' remarked Lovell; 'but I cannot help understanding Miss Vere's allusions, and I suppose they mean that you're engaged to be married to Mr Blythe. Is that the case, Miss Leyton?'

'Well, not exactly.'

'Is it only her nonsense?'

'Not exactly,' she repeated, growing more confused.

'Do tell me the truth, then! You don't know how much it means to me.'

'We—that is, Mr Blythe and I—have talked of such a thing, but mother doesn't think that father will ever give his consent to it.'

'And do you wish him to do so, Miss Leyton? Does your happiness depend on it?'

'I am not quite sure.'

'But if you cared for Blythe, you *would* be quite sure. You could have no doubt upon the subject.'

'He is fond of me,' said Alice.

'There is nothing wonderful in that.

Plenty of people must be fond of you. The question is, *Are you fond of him ?*'

'I don't think you should ask me such a question, Captain Lovell.'

'Forgive me if I have said too much. I would not offend you for the world. But — but—I am very unhappy about it !'

'So am I,' whispered Alice.

'If that is the case,' exclaimed the captain, seizing her hand, 'come to some understanding about it at once! Speak to Mrs Leyton and Mr Blythe on the subject, and let me know the worst. For this suspense is intolerable, Alice : it is killing me by inches.'

'Hush!' said Alice quickly, withdrawing her hand ; 'be quiet, for goodness' sake, Captain Lovell. Here is Jack.'

And indeed at that very moment Vernon Blythe appeared round the wheel-house, whistling as he went. He smiled pleasantly as he came in sight of Alice, and took no notice whatever of her crimson face and flurried manner. He nodded to Captain Lovell, who was confusedly striking a fusee on the heel of his boot, in order to light a cigar, and remarking, ' Lucky fellow, to be able to smoke when you choose. I wish my time had come,' turned away as light-heartedly as if it had been some other man's betrothed whom he had detected in a flirtation behind the wheel-house.

' Did he see us, do you think ? ' asked Alice fearfully of her companion, as Jack disappeared.

' Well, I really think he must have *seen* us,' replied the captain deliberately, ' for we are both full size, you know ! But he appeared very pleasant about it.'

' Oh, dear ! ' exclaimed Alice, ' I hope he did *not* see us.'

' You are afraid of him, then ? ' remarked Lovell.

' No, not afraid, only—he would think so badly of me.'

' And you wish him to think well of you.'

'Oh, I don't know *what* I wish,' cried the girl, in a voice that was very suspicious of tears.

The passengers had retreated below. There was no one but themselves on deck, except, indeed, Mr Coffin, whose back was turned to them, and the man at the wheel, who was shut up in his box, and could only look straight before him.

'Shall I tell you what *I* wish,' whispered Captain Lovell, as his arm stole round her waist ; '*I* have no doubt upon the matter, Alice.'

'No! no! I cannot hear—I do not want to hear!' exclaimed the girl nervously, as she jumped up from her seat and ran down to the saloon, leaving the captain to finish the flirtation by himself.

CHAPTER V.

THE GLASS FALLS.

HREE days after the events re-
lated in the last chapter, the
trade winds, which had escorted
the *Pandora* so well on her passage, died
away, and left the vessel in a dead calm,
till a snorting southerly breeze came over
the ocean, and sent her careering along
at her best pace.

The wind which rattled through the
rigging was cold and chilly, and made
the ladies unpack their furs, and huddle
round the stove. Few patronised the
deck—the air was too keen and searching.

It was a marvellous change from the sultry weather of the week before, when Alice Leyton had sat with Captain Lovell under the wheel-house, and most of the passengers felt it acutely.

A huge purple bank, lined with silver, had risen upon the beam, and the sun assumed a watery and unnatural appearance.

Mr Coffin, indifferent to everything but the welfare of the vessel, kept a look-out upon the poop, anxiously watching at intervals the ominous-looking cloud, which was gradually growing larger. With his cap drawn down closely over his eyes, his thick, bull-dog neck encircled by a red worsted muffler, a big quid stuck in his cheeks, and his rough, broad hands embedded in his trousers pockets, he was the model of a British seaman.

But he was by no means morose or ill-tempered. Exceedingly shy and reserved, from ignorance of the ways and manners of society, he seldom commenced a conversation, but if any of the passengers were bold enough to speak to him, they found him unpolished, but kindly in disposition. Under his weather-beaten exterior he hid a warm, good heart, for Mr Coffin had a soul of honour, and a mean or cowardly action would have been utterly beneath him.

'Good-morning; nice day this, isn't it?' remarked Godfrey Harland.

'Yes, sir,' replied the chief officer; 'but I am afraid we are going to have a blow. I don't like the looks of it.'

'It looks dirty to windward, I must say. Do you think there is mischief in that bank?

'I am sure there is,' said Coffin; 'we shall have to shorten down before daybreak, but it won't be much. The glass is falling, too, sir, and perhaps you know the old saying,—

"When the glass falls low, prepare for a blow,
When the glass rises high, let all your kites fly."

But we shall be prepared. I have the

hands up at the fore and main reefing the tackles and spilling lines, and the chain tacks and double sheets are on.'

'What are they doing to your main-topgallant parcell?' inquired Harland, looking up aloft at the sailors at work.

'Well, they are lacing on some new leather parcelling,' replied the mate solemnly, stroking his chin. 'The old stuff don't let the yard travel quick enough for my liking. But, if I'm not very much mistaken, this is not your first voyage, sir,' he continued, fixing his keen eyes upon Harland's face.

'Oh, no,' replied the other lightly; 'I have often been on the briny. I owned a yacht in New York once—an eighty-tonner—and all my nautical knowledge was learned aboard her.'

'Was she square-rigged,' asked Mr Coffin indifferently.

'No; fore and aft. As nice a little craft as ever you saw, and, by the holy poker, she could sail too. There were few to beat her.'

' How do you come, then, to know about maintopgallant parcells, if she wasn't square-rigged ?' demanded the chief officer, looking full at him.

Harland felt he was caught in his own trap. He had foolishly acknowledged that the only vessel he had sailed in was a moderate-sized yacht, which could have been stowed away, with twenty others, in the *Pandora's* hold, and that all his sea knowledge was gained aboard of her. How, then, could he possibly know the names, and understand the use, of gear which was never seen on such small craft ?

After spluttering out an unintelligible excuse, he attempted to smooth the matter over by inviting his companion to join him in a glass of grog. But the old sea-dog gruffly refused his offer, and turning away, with a mysterious ' Humph,' sent a long squirt of red tobacco juice straight into the stern sheets of the lifeboat.

When Harland noticed his altered manner, he sidled away under the lee of the pilot-house, whilst Mr Coffin, after scanning the horizon and satisfying himself that there was nothing in sight, leaned against the taffrail, and thought to himself that— 'Mr Harland was a darned sight too deep for most people, but he had taken him flat aback that time.'

At mid-day the captain shot the sun— a feat which Mr Horace Greenwood came up on deck expressly to see, and was much disappointed when Jack Blythe informed him he was just a minute too late; and by that time the wind had increased a little, blowing from south-west to south-south-west in sudden gusts, and the fore and mizen royals, and the smaller stay sails were made fast.

Alice Leyton, in a dark brown travel-ling ulster, and a felt hat trimmed with a dainty tuft of feathers, which blew about with the wind, and mingled with her sunny curls, had left the close saloon for the open

air, and now stood leaning against the
wheel-house, holding on her hat with one
hand, whilst the breeze caught her skirts
and wound them tightly round her supple
figure.

'Why, Alice,' exclaimed Jack, as he
came up to her, 'what a brave girl you
are to venture on deck! But don't be
blown away. We can't spare you yet, you
know,' and he passed his arm round her
waist to steady her as he spoke.

Alice shrank palpably from his embrace.

'Don't, Jack, please. I can stand very
well by myself, and some one may be
looking.'

'No one is looking, my dear, and if
they were, nothing could be more natural
than for me to proffer my assistance to a
young female in distress on such a windy
day.'

'I'm not in distress,' replied Alice, half
ready to cry at the situation.

'Oh, yes, you are. You don't know

what a south-wester is yet. Your petticoats will be over your head in another
minute.'

'Oh,' cried the girl involuntarily, as her
hand left her hat to travel down to her
skirts. 'Jack, let me go back to the
saloon at once. I don't want to stay here
any longer.'

'Indeed I won't. I see you very
seldom now, and I mean to make the
most of the opportunity. How long is it
since you kissed me? At least three
weeks. Don't you think if you brought
your face a little nearer this way, you
wouldn't feel the wind so much? Your
cheeks are getting positively crimson
with it. You'd better take advantage
of my offer, and shelter under my lee.'

'No, no!' exclaimed Alice, half in fun
and half in earnest, 'I don't want to kiss
you, Jack. I can manage much better by
myself.'

'Or with the help of Captain Lovell,' he
answered. 'Isn't that true, Alice? It

isn't the help that's disagreeable to you, it's the helper.'

'Oh, Jack, how can you say such a thing, when we've known each other for so long?'

'Perhaps we've known each other *too* long, and have come to know each other too well, Alice. However, I won't tease you. I've often refused your kisses, so it's only fair you should have the option of refusing mine now and then. And I suppose you're tired of them. It's no wonder.'

Alice did not know what to say. She longed to tell him the truth, but she dared not. She was too fond of him to care to see his bright face clouded by disappointment, and yet she knew now that she could never marry him. Oh dear, she sighed to herself, what should she do?

'Jack,' she commenced timidly, 'I think you'd soon be sick of me. I don't think I'm a very nice girl. In fact, I'm *sure* I'm not. And I shall make a worse wife.

I've almost made up my mind never to marry at all.'

Jack burst out laughing. He had known it would come to this at last. He had watched the confession drawing nearer day by day. And he was not sorry for it. Only he determined that Alice should not have it all her own way. He must have some fun out of her first.

'What are you talking about?' he replied, with affected earnestness. 'You are a great deal too modest, my darling. You'll make the very best and sweetest wife in all the world. *I'm* the proper judge of that. Besides, don't forget that you are pledged to me, and no power on earth will make me release you from your promise.'

Alice sighed audibly, and looked over the sea.

'But would it be right, Jack,' she said presently, 'for me to marry, if I knew I could not fulfil the duties of a wife?'

'Much you know about the duties of a

wife !' exclaimed Jack merrily. 'You can fulfil all *I* shall require from you : I'll take my oath of that.'

' Mother says,' continued Alice solemnly, 'that I am utterly unfit for any of the graver requirements of life, and that when my father sees how frivolous and pleasure-seeking I am, he is sure to refuse his con-sent to my leaving home.'

'Ah! I can guess now what has brought this serious fit upon you, Alice. Your mother has been frightening you with regard to what Mr Leyton may say to our engagement. But don't you be afraid, dear. If he should make my position an objection to our immediate marriage, I'll leave you in his care till I shall have attained higher rank and better pay. And, meanwhile, you can be learning your duties as a wife,' said Jack slyly.

' How can I learn with no one to teach me ?' replied Alice sharply. ' Besides, Jack, it may be years and years before you get promotion! Am I to be an old maid all that time?'

'Why, I thought you were never going to marry at all just now,' said her lover. 'You are only just eighteen, Alice. Surely a few years—say till you're five-and-twenty—would not be too long to wait for such happiness as ours will be? It isn't as if you were going to marry Captain Lovell, you know, or some common-place fellow of that sort. I will serve for you as Jacob did for Rachel, and if I can wait seven years for you, surely you will do no less for me, eh?'

'Oh, no! of course not,' replied the girl, who had the greatest difficulty to keep the tears back from her eyes. 'But —but I think I'd rather go down to the saloon, Jack, this wind is so horribly strong it makes my eyes water.'

'All right, if you wish it, but I must tow you safely to the door,' replied Jack, as he took her across the deck and saw her disappear in the depths of the saloon cabin, without speaking another word to him.

'Poor little girl,' he thought, as he turned laughing away, 'she's terribly puzzled to know what to say to me. She would have liked to scratch out my eyes for that remark about Lovell, only she didn't dare. Well, it'll come out sooner or later, but it's not my business to help her make the confession. If she gives me up of her own free will, I shall thank God. But if this is only a passing fancy on her part or *his*, I must go through with it.' And Vernon Blythe sighed as heavily at the prospect as Alice Leyton had done, as he went to his work.

CHAPTER VI.

TO THE RESCUE.

ALICE flew into the saloon, with her eyes brimful of tears, and the first person she encountered was Captain Lovell, who regarded her with looks of the utmost concern. He was a handsome man, in the ordinary acceptation of the term, of about thirty, the sort of man to catch the fancy of a woman who loved her lover's face before his spirit, but there was no soul in the expression of his face, and no sentiment in his disposition. Any other

girl would probably have done as well
for him as Alice Leyton, had he been
thrown in her society for several weeks
consecutively, but on the other hand Alice
would do as well for him as any other
woman, and was happily of a tempera-
ment that would never arrive at a
knowledge of the truth. At present, she
thought Robert Lovell delightful. He
never corrected her, as Jack too often
did. He was never *distrait* when she
chattered to him, or wrapped in his own
thoughts. He never gazed dreamily at
the stars, or made remarks that were
utterly beyond her comprehension. And
so she quite imagined she was in love,
and so, perhaps, she was. As Captain
Lovell saw her tear-stained cheeks, he
begged her confidence.

'What is the matter, Miss Leyton?
Has any one dared to annoy you?'

'Oh, no! It is nothing. Only—only
—Mr Blythe teases me so. He says—'

'I can guess it all. You need go no

further. He presses you on the subject
of your engagement to him.'

'Yes. He says he will never release
me,' replied Alice, checking a sob.

'Alice! we must put an end to this
at once. It is worrying you too much.
May I speak to your mother, dearest?
Have I your leave to say that we love
each other, and ask her to consent to
our marriage?'

'If—if—she won't tell Jack,' whispered Alice fearfully. 'I should be afraid
to be on the same ship with him, if he
knew.'

'My darling! Do you suppose you
are not safe with *me*? — that any one
would be permitted to hurt you, whilst
I am by your side? However, that is
a matter for after consideration. May
I go now and speak to your mother?'

'If you wish it,' replied Alice, as she
ran away to the shelter of her own
cabin.

The afternoon was far advanced, and

the wind had freshened into a loud, continuous blast.

In the saloon, the passengers of the
Pandora, now quite accustomed to her
varied pranks, were seated at the long
table, amusing themselves according to
their several tastes and proclivities.
Some were playing at cards, chess, or
dominoes; others were reading, or trying to write letters; whilst a few of
the younger ones were gathered round
the piano to hear Miss Vere and Miss
Vansittart sing.

All around them the waves tossed
and tumbled; the wind howled with a
dismal monotony, like a dog baying at
the moon; and the rain hissed and
spluttered on the deck, and against the
closed portholes. Now and then, far
above the confusion of the elements,
might be heard the scream of a sea-
gull, as, scared by the rapid approach of
the monstrous waves that threatened to
engulf it, it flew in terror from its watery

bed, to describe terrified circles in the murky air. Falling glass, broken china, and an occasional bump, as the vessel gave a lurch, and some one who had not quite acquired his sea-legs came down in a sitting position, were the order of the day, and those passengers who had secured a comfortable seat felt it was wiser not to leave it. Mrs Leyton, a fair, soft-looking woman, was stretched out at full length on one of the saloon sofas, covered with wraps and shawls, and with little Winnie (her baby) lying fast asleep by her side, as Captain Lovell made his way up to her.

'We are going to have a dreadful night, Captain Lovell, I am afraid,' she said, as he paused beside her couch. 'My poor baby is quite tired with tumbling about, and has fallen asleep. Do you know where my Alice is? She said she was going on deck a little while ago, but I'm sure it is not fit weather for her to be out. She is such a careless, thoughtless thing. Fancy! if she were blown overboard!'

'Heaven forbid!' cried Captain Lovell suddenly. 'But you may feel quite easy about her. She has just gone to her berth.'

'Ah! I thought she would soon have enough of it; but girls are so self-willed now-a-days. It is a great responsibility to have a grown-up daughter. I shall be thankful when Mr Leyton can share it with me. How terrible the wind sounds as it moans through the shrouds!' observed Mrs Leyton, shuddering.

'I trust you are not frightened,' said Captain Lovell. 'The sound is the worst part about it.'

'Oh, yes, I know there is no danger; but we women are timid creatures, and generally behave badly on such occasions.'

'I think Miss Leyton behaves beautifully. Even in that sharp squall we had the other day, her cheek never blanched, nor did she lose her spirits.'

'Ah, Alice does not know what fear is. I wish sometimes she had a more wholesome dread of consequences. But she has always had her own way with me, and I am quite afraid when we get to Dunedin that my husband will say I have been too lenient.'

'May I enlist your sympathies on my behalf before you meet Mr Leyton?' said the captain, taking a seat beside her. 'It is of Alice—of Miss Leyton, I should say—that I wished to speak to you, and she has given me permission to do so. We love each other, Mrs Leyton. Will you plead our cause with your husband, and gain his consent to our marriage?'

Mrs Leyton sat up on the sofa in her surprise, and little Winnie gave a fretful cry at being disturbed.

'Alice has encouraged you to speak to me, Captain Lovell? But she considers herself engaged to be married to Mr Vernon Blythe. It is not a match I could ever approve of, because the young man has no settled income, but they were much thrown together at Southsea, and settled the matter between themselves without consulting me. I had no idea that she had changed her mind. Are you *quite* sure you are following her wishes in joining her name to your own ?'

'I can only tell you that I asked her permission to address you on this sub- ject ten minutes ago, and that she gave it me most graciously. The fact is, Mrs Leyton, Alice has often spoken to me of her half-engagement to Mr Blythe with deep regret. She declares nothing will induce her to marry him, and that—God bless her !—she has every intention of marrying *me*, subject (of course) to the consent of her parents.'

'Well, I really can't understand her, and I must decline to have anything to do with the matter,' replied Mrs Leyton, lying back again upon her pillows. 'I really don't know what the girls are made

of now-a-days. The scenes Alice subjected me to when she first fell in love
with young Blythe were beyond concep-
tion. She was going to die, or go mad,
straight off, if she couldn't be engaged
to him. And so, to quiet her, I gave a
sort of reluctant consent. But I confess
I hadn't the least idea the young man
would come out in the same ship with
us. And now it seems she's in love
with *you*. And what excuse does she
intend to offer Mr Blythe for her conduct ? '

' I think Miss Leyton hopes that *you*
may be persuaded to manage so delicate
a matter for her, and let the young gentleman know that she desires to be released
from her engagement to him,' said Captain Lovell sheepishly.

' I shall do no such thing, sir. Alice
must conduct her love affairs herself.
Such a task would be altogether too
much for my nerves ; for though I do
not consider Vernon Blythe an eligible

suitor for my daughter, I like the young
fellow excessively. So if his affections
and his pride are to be wounded through
my daughter, she can do it herself. I
refuse to open my lips to him, and I
must say I think he has been treated
very badly.'

'My dear Mrs Leyton, do make some
allowance for Alice's feelings. Our hearts
are not completely under our own control,
remember. Love is not to be coerced,
like any baser passion.'

'Well, I hope you'll bear that in
mind, Captain Lovell, if you should ever
be my daughter's husband, and catch her
flirting with some other man. And don't
make too sure she'll stick to you. A girl
that changes once may change twice.
And I don't know that Mr Leyton will
accept your offer for her more than the
other. He's got no romance about him,
and looks high for his daughter.

'He could not look *too* high for such
a pearl as Alice. I shall like him all the

better for that,' replied Captain Lovell.
'But won't you be persuaded to break the
news to Mr Blythe for us?'

'No! I absolutely refuse, and it's no
use your asking me,' returned Mrs Leyton,
who was really fond of Jack. 'If Alice
wishes him to know she's a jilt, she can
tell him so herself.'

'You are *too* hard upon her,' murmured
the captain, as he withdrew from the
interview, feeling much less light hearted
than he had done at the commencement.
But before the next day was over both he
and Alice had experienced a shock which
made their own troubles sink into insig-
nificance beside it.

After a tempestuous night, a long white
streak far away in the southward pro-
claimed the break of dawn. The sky was
clear, and the stars flickered with waning
light in the spangled heavens. The gale,
which had blown with great fury during
the night, was abating with the coming of
day, and Blythe, who well knew that it

would die away as quickly as it had sprung up, hoisted the topsails as soon as it showed signs of dropping. The storm clouds were dispersed by the sun, which tinted the sky with orange and crimson hues, and the moon, paling beneath the stronger light, disappeared in solemn stateliness behind her vast curtain of cerulean drapery. The waves still leapt and growled with impotent rage, but, deserted by the wind and beaten down with the rain, their energy was almost expended.

The *Pandora* laboured against the turbulent sea, like a horse stumbling over a freshly-ploughed field. At times she took large spoonfuls over her forechains, greatly to the annoyance of the black cook, who had continually to clear his scupper holes with a long caul, and to push away the cinders which choked them up and prevented the water from escaping. Now and again the vessel dashed on to the top of a swell, and the sea rushed from her in boiling surf; then she would rise over a mountainous wave as if about to make another desperate plunge, till her stern went with a rude swash into the sea, sending thousands of bubbling whirlpools hissing in her wake, whilst the shore-folk turned uneasily in their bunks, and wished it were time to rise.

At eight bells the maintopgallant sail was sheeted home, and the outer jib run up. After which the *Pandora* behaved in a more graceful and lady-like manner, and when the decks had been 'squeegeed' down, all hands emerged from their close quarters to enjoy the invigorating air, which the ocean had rendered still more grateful by a flavouring of brine.

The day became warmer, the wind hauled round to the northward and east-ward, and the sun, casting off his sickly appearance, shone forth with a cheerful warmth.

Alice Leyton, under the escort of Captain Lovell, walked the lee side of the deck. They were discussing together the details of Lovell's interview with Mrs Leyton the evening before, and the girl looked both unhappy and dismayed, as she heard the remarks her mother had made upon her conduct.

Mr Vansittart and Godfrey Harland, who appeared by general consent to be considered as *fiancé* to Grace Vansittart, conversed at the foot of the mizenmast, and a weather cloth was spread in the lower rigging for the benefit of the ladies, who took advantage of its shelter for their camp-stools and wicker-chairs. On the wheel-house benches were seated two or three young officers, who were holding an animated discussion on the probable advent of a Conservative administration, while Miss Vere and Mr Fowler, with Harold Greenwood (who had entirely succumbed to the charms of the fair actress) close at hand, were lounging on the skylight.

Suddenly—in the midst of the buzz

of conversation and the sound of laughter —came a low, piteous cry, that seemed to rend the air, and spread from one end of the ship to the other. Then a long, deep nautical shout from the maintop bawled out the terrifying words,—'*Man overboard!*' In a moment, the whole deck resembled a disturbed anthill, and Mr Coffin ran aft to the wheel.

'Put your helm a-port, man!' he cried, seizing the spokes and putting them down ; and then in the same breath he shouted, 'Cut away that life-buoy!'

When the feeble cry was first heard, Alice and Captain Lovell ran to the side of the vessel, whence the sound of a sudden splash had caught their ears. Peering into the water, they saw nothing at first but a small bundle of clothes, but in another moment a velvet cloak and a 'granny' bonnet to match came plainly in view—the cloak and the bonnet of Winnie Leyton. Alice turned white and sick with horror.

' My God !' she cried, ' it is our baby !
She is drowning! She will die! Will
no one save her? Let me go,' she continued, struggling violently in the detain-
ing grasp of Captain Lovell, who feared
lest in her agony she should jump overboard after her sister.

' Don't be afraid, dearest,' he urged.
' It will be all right. See! they are
getting out a boat. They will pick her
up in a minute. Pray, *pray* don't do
anything rash,' he said, as he attempted
to lead her away.

As she turned, she encountered Jack
Blythe, who was already stripped to his
shirt and trousers.

' Jack! save her!' she screamed.

' Never fear, Alice! I will bring her
back to you,' he answered. ' D—n it,
man, stand on one side!' he shouted to
Lovell, as he clutched him violently, and
threw him against the astonished bystanders.

' What the d—' commenced Lovell,

but in another second Jack Blythe, gird-
ing up his muscular young figure for
the effort, had sprung over the side of
the *Pandora* to the rescue of Winifred
Leyton.

CHAPTER VII.

FREE.

HE foreyard was pointed, and the gear of the mainsail hauled up, while Richard Sparkes, with the aid of five hands, swung the lifeboat into its davits. On the poop deck there was terrible confusion. The married ladies crowded round poor Mrs Leyton, who was half swooning from her anxiety and fear; Alice, refusing all assistance from Captain Lovell or anybody else, stood with clenched teeth and strained eyeballs watching the two black specks that bobbed up and down like corks upon the water ; and the rest of the passengers pressed against the taffrail, talking in loud and excited tones to each other, whilst they watched the fight for life or death.

In a few minutes the boat was pushed off, and the sturdy sailors made the oars bend beneath the weight of their arms. Mr Sparkes held the tiller, and kept cheering on the men, whilst he eagerly watched the objects ahead of them.

What a long, long time it seemed. The boat did not appear to gain a dozen yards, as it plunged and tossed against the billows. But the seamen had muscles that had been developed by climbing and hauling. All their sinews were like springs of steel. Each man, with one foot firmly planted against the thwart in front of him, lay back upon his oar, with a long, sweeping, steady English stroke, till his head was nearly parallel with his companion's knee—a stretch that would have made a Dutchman look on with awe, mingled

with admiration, and a pull that sent the
boat's stem through the rollers, cutting
them like a knife, and plumping her down
with a heavy bump on the other side.
Vernon Blythe and the child were now
fully a mile astern. He had managed to
grasp the life-buoy, which was a good
thing for both of them, for poor little
Winnie clung convulsively round his
throat, entirely impeding his swimming,
whilst she sobbed and gasped, as she
tried to recover her breath after the
nauseous doses of salt water she had
swallowed.

She was a pretty little creature, and
just at that age when children become
quaint and interesting. Her brown hair—
which curled naturally, like that of her
elder sister—now hung in a wet clinging
mass about her face and shoulders. The
gay 'granny' bonnet was gone: it had
floated far away to leeward. The velvet
cloak still hung tightly about her, and
added considerably to her weight. Her

little fat and shapely legs, enveloped in
long Hessian boots, now shuddering and
almost stiff with cold, rested on Jack
Blythe's hips.   It was a hard struggle
for him to keep her above water, for
the terrified child nearly choked him, and
he was exhausted from swimming in the
boisterous, choppy sea, that kept on
breaking in a remorseless lather over his
head and face, and prevented him from
breathing freely.

'Don't—cry—baby.   There's—a—boat
—coming,' he gasped; but the little one
did not answer him, except by a heart-
rending sob, and a tighter pressure on
his throat.

Swish—h—h went the lifeboat, as the
dripping oars were lifted, feathered, and
dipped again.   The shellbacks, in regular
time, gave a muffled deep sigh, as they
are wont to do after the tremendous
exertion of a stiff pull.   Click-clack went
the rollocks, as they shied and swerved
in their sockets—a long whirr-r—the

order given '*Rowed all*'—a rumbling
noise, as the oars were shipped on the
thwarts, and the baby and her preserver
were lifted by strong arms from the embrace of the treacherous ocean, and hauled
safely into the boat.

'Now, give way, lads, merrily,' said
Sparkes, as Vernon Blythe seated himself
with the youngster on his knee, and the
wiry saltfish, with a cheer for the second
officer, set themselves with renewed vigour
to their task. They had warmed to their
work by this time. The perspiration
stood in large beads upon their foreheads,
and their blades went forward in clock-
work time. Little Winifred, with her
head resting upon Vernon's breast, gave
vent to plaintive sobs, burying her face
in the wet folds of the young sailor's
shirt, and at intervals peeping out as the
Pandora hove-to in the distance.

'Ship—wouldn't—wait—for baby,' she
said, whimpering, as she glanced up into
Jack's face.

'She will now,' replied Vernon, smiling;
'you went too fast for the poor ship, baby,
but she stopped as soon as ever she found
you had tumbled overboard. Poor mite,'
he added kindly, as he kissed her scared
face; 'it was a narrow shave for you.'

'Brother Jack found me,' said Winnie,
with another little sob.

Her sister had taught her to call him
'*brother*' long ago at Southsea, and as
Vernon heard her now, he smiled almost
sadly, to think how prematurely the ap-
pellation had been applied.

The passengers had crowded at the side
of the vessel to watch the issue of the
accident, and saw the drowning child and
Vernon lifted into the lifeboat with the
utmost satisfaction. Some of them were
cheering vociferously and waving their
pocket handkerchiefs to express their joy,
whilst others were shouting '*Bravo!*' But
Vernon Blythe sat in the stern, heedless of
their congratulations. He was thinking of
Winnie's narrow escape from a watery

grave,—of Alice Leyton's agonised expression when she appealed to him to save her sister, and he felt thankful that he had been made the instrument of the little one's safety. It seemed as though he had thereby paid part of the debt he owed to Alice, and found it so difficult to discharge. Each painful incident he had just undergone passed in rapid confusion through his mind. He recalled how Alice had been talking by the fiferail with Captain Lovell, when the cry of ‘ *Man overboard !* ’ had been raised, and he had seen the baby quickly floating astern,—how he had knocked that gentleman into the arms of the bystanders as he jumped to her rescue, — then the leap from the half-round,—the cold immersion,—the sight of the majestic vessel as she sailed away from them,—the piteous crying of little Winnie, —his strenuous efforts to obtain the life-buoy, with the child clinging to him for dear life, and the horrible thought that they would both be drowned clasped thus together. Just as his thoughts had reached their climax, they were disturbed. Bump went the boat against the iron side, the tackles were overhauled, and hooked on, and three of the sailors, with the aid of a line and the mainbrace, clambered on to the deck. Hand-over-hand the slack was hauled in, and the heads of the crew appeared above the rail.

Then the order was given to ' Belay,' and Vernon Blythe, with the child still clinging to him, stepped on board again. The quarter-deck was crowded. Everybody wished to congratulate him, and embrace little Winnie ; a dozen hands were stretched out to grasp his own. But Jack had no time to attend to anybody. He strode past all the faces that beamed upon him, until he had reached the side of Mrs Leyton, and placed her child upon her lap.

'Oh, Jack! my dear boy, how shall we ever thank you?' cried the poor mother hysterically, as she clasped her baby in her arms.

'By saying nothing about it, Mrs Leyton,' he answered cheerily; 'you know I would have done as much for any one of you, twice over.'

'My darling Winnie!' exclaimed Alice, as she smothered her little sister's face in kisses. 'What should we have done if we had lost you?'

'Brother Jack picked me out of the water,' said Winnie, who had begun to realise she was safe, and might leave off crying.

At that name, Alice blushed scarlet.

'Give her to me, mother,' she said hurriedly; 'I must change her clothes at once.'

'Yes, Miss Alice, and put her in a hot bath, and then into bed until to-morrow morning,' interposed Dr Lennard, 'or she will be ill.'

'I will, doctor; come, darling,' continued Alice, as she seized Winnie in her arms, and without noticing Jack, or giving him one word of thanks, passed through the crowd into the cabin passage, and out of sight. She was too conscience-stricken to be able to trust herself to thank him for his bravery. But Jack, who had been looking forward to her expressions of gratitude for the risk he had run on her sister's behalf, only thought she under-rated it, and gazed after her in disappointed silence.

'Come, Blythe! how do *you* feel?' inquired Dr Lennard, shaking him by the arm; 'you must not get sleepy, you know.'

'Oh, I'm all right, doctor, thank you, and none the worse for my swim, though it was plaguey cold, I can tell you.'

'You must come with me and have a pick-me-up,' said the doctor.

'No, thanks, sir! don't trouble about me! A good stiff glass of grog and a change of linen are all I want.'

'Well, go and strip off those wet togs then, my boy, whilst I mix a steaming jorum for you,' replied Dr Lennard. 'You've done a good day's work, Blythe, and we mustn't let you suffer for it. Come along at once,' and he pulled the young officer away with him.

When both Jack and the baby had disappeared, and the passengers had discussed the adventure in all its bearings, their excitement toned down, and they returned to their usual avocations, whilst the *Pandora*, with her mainsail set, sailed on at seven knots an hour.

But in the afternoon, when little Winnie was wrapt in peaceful slumber, and Jack was on deck attending to his duty, Alice Leyton came up to him, with flushed cheeks and outstretched hands.

'Jack,' she said (and her voice seemed unaccountably tender to him, after the somewhat frivolous manner in which she had treated him of late), 'we have so much to thank you for, we don't know how to do it. I hope you did not think it unkind of me not to come before, but mother has been quite ill from the shock and the excitement, and there has been no one to look

after baby but myself. It was so
courageous—so brave—so good of you
to peril your life for—for—'

'Pray don't say another word about it,
Alice. It was only my duty, and there
was but little danger. Any man in my
position would have done the same.'

'But no man *did*,' she answered quickly ; 'all the rest stood by like sheep. The
only one beside yourself who rendered
the least assistance was Mr Fowler, who
cut away the life-buoy, and threw it
overboard.'

'They were not in my position, Alice.
Think how long we have been friends.
Do you suppose I could have looked on
to see any one whom you care for drown ?
I thought you had a better opinion of
me than that.'

'I think you are the best and the kind-
est and the bravest friend I ever had,'
replied Alice, with a sob in her throat;
'and if I could only repay you—but that
is impossible—but if I could only show you

some kindness, in return for all you have
done for us to-day, I should be so happy.'

'You *can* repay me amply,' said Jack,
'and that is by being open with me, Alice.
I know that you have something on your
mind which you are unwilling to confide
to me.   This is not as it should be.
Friends in our position should trust each
other *all in all or not at all.* If you
consider that you owe me any return
for your sister's safety, give it me in your
confidence.'

'Oh, Jack! how *shall* I tell you?
sobbed Alice.   'You are so sweet and
good.   I admire and I love you so much
—and yet—and yet—'

'Shall I try and help you, dear? When
baby found herself in my arms, she whimpered *"Brother Jack picked me up!"*
I think *that* is the name you would like
to call me by, as well as baby. I think
you want me to be *"Brother Jack"* to
you.'

'Oh, Vernon! have you *guessed?*' cried

Alice, turning her crimson face away from him.

'That you would be quite ready to accept Lovell's addresses were you only freed from mine? Yes, Alice. I have guessed as much as that. Am I right?'

'But won't it—won't it *hurt* you?' she whispered.

'Not very much. My vanity may suffer a little, but that is wholesome discipline. And I have feared, too, for some time past, that we were not *quite* suited to each other; so you see it will be for the best after all. Only, Alice, we must always be friends,' he continued, as he held out his hand.

'Oh, yes, Jack—*dear* Jack!' she answered, with her bright eyes swimming in tears; 'and sometimes I think—sometimes I almost wish—'

'Think and wish nothing, Alice, except what concerns yourself and Captain Lovell,' interposed Jack, who had a wholesome horror of a sentimental scene in public, and was somewhat afraid also of what she might be going to say. 'He seems a very good sort of fellow to me, and I have no doubt he will make you happy. And you may rely on my good wishes, not only for the wedding, but all your future life. And now, good-bye, dear, for I have business below. Give my love to your mother, and tell her how thankful I am for baby's safety, and how glad that both your hearts are set at rest.'

He waved his hand gaily to her as he disappeared, and Alice believed he was merely acting a part to hide his disappointment.

But (had she known it) his heart was far lighter than his action. A load had been lifted off it. He felt—for the first time—that he was free (in all honour) to woo and win Iris Hetherley!

CHAPTER VIII.

CONFIDENCES.

MANY landsmen may wonder why vessels bound south go so far to the westward, instead of making a direct course through the tropics. It is because the trades are so much stronger on the other side that they adopt the longer route, in order to make a quicker passage.

For the same reason, the *Pandora*, after skirting the coast of Brazil, sailed as far south as fifty-two degrees, that is, six hundred miles to the south of the Cape of Good Hope, where the westerly breezes could be depended on.

As the ship drew nearer the Antarctic regions, the weather became colder. The 'boatswains' and 'boobies' were left astern, and black - speckled Cape pigeons and snowy albatrosses were to be seen in their stead. The lively skipjacks, bright-coloured bonitas, and swift dolphins had all disappeared, but monster whales, that swam majestically after the vessel, denoting their presence by squirting up volumes of water through their blow-holes, and boisterous porpoises, that gambolled under the boom, and indulged in clumsy antics, supplied the deficiency. The sky wore a leaden appearance. The air was exhilarating, and the wind sharp and keen. No one complained now of the oppressive heat. The ladies packed away their fans again, and came on deck in their furs. The sailors no longer ran about in white ducks and with bare feet, but put on strong Cunarders, pilot trousers, and sea-boots.

And all hands hailed the change with

gladness.   The heat at times had made
the passengers both languid and discontented.   It was difficult to rest either by
day or night in the hot and stuffy saloon
or the close cabins.   But now they felt
compelled to be on the move.   The
stove was surrounded all day by a flock
of petticoats, and at night the dead lights
were firmly screwed up to prevent the
chilly air from penetrating the sleeping
berths.   On one of these raw evenings
few ventured to show their faces on deck.
Some of the ladies were sitting with the
card players in the smoking-room, a small
party was · assembled in Vernon's berth
speculating on *rouge - et - noir*, and two
women, seated in the second cabin, were
engaged in earnest conversation.   They
were Maggie Greet and Iris Harland.
The servant was seated at her mistress's
feet, with her hands firmly clasped on
Iris's knees as she looked up into her
beautiful face and told her story.   It had
taken Maggie a long time to summon

up courage to confide the news of her
engagement to Will Farrell to her friend
and mistress. For some unaccountable
reason, the girl had felt strangely shy
about disclosing her good fortune, and
she might not have confessed it even
now, had not something occurred connected with it, which she felt it in-
cumbent that Iris should know. But
she told the tale with such a burning
face, and so many interruptions, that her
hearer could only imagine she was too
happy to be coherent.

'Oh, my dear,' Iris exclaimed, when
she had at last arrived at a knowledge
of the facts, 'I *am* so glad! And you
have been engaged to Mr Farrell for
a whole ˙ fortnight, and never told
me of it? What a naughty girl!
Didn't you know that I should be the
very first to congratulate you on your
good luck? For you *are* very lucky,
you know, Maggie. Fancy, finding a
husband before you even touch land!

And such a good one too! For I am *sure* Mr Farrell will be good to you, my dear! He has a true face, and you will be a happy woman! I am very, *very* glad.'

And Iris stooped down, and kissed Maggie's forehead.

'Oh, don't do that!' cried the girl hurriedly. 'I ain't worthy of it, mistress, nor of nothing that's happened to me neither, and I've told Will as much. Only he's good enough to overlook all my faults, and say he'll take me as I am. And you'll come and live with us, won't you, my pretty? We'll all go straight up into the bush as soon as ever we land, and there I'll work to my life's end to try and make you comfortable and happy.'

'My dear Maggie,' remonstrated Iris, 'you forget. Mr Harland is on board, and I have taken this step to be with him. It is an immense load off my mind to think you are so happily provided for,

for I have always been fearful lest he should resent your having accompanied me; but my place is by his side, and as soon as ever we come in sight of land, I shall walk boldly up to him and declare myself. I hate the thought of it,' continued Iris, with the tears in her soft eyes. 'I despise him, and I fear him. But it is his business to maintain me, and my right to demand support from him, and I mean to have it.'

'But, mistress,' said Maggie, in an earnest tone, 'you *mustn't* go with him. It isn't safe. He is a *bad* man—ah, much worse than you've ever thought of! —and he'd kill you as soon as look at you if you happened to be in his way. Don't think of it any more. He's made you miserable all along, and he'll make you miserable again. Come with Will and me, and forget all about that brute. And after a while, perhaps, you'll meet with some one as will make you *really* happy, and then all the past will look like a bad dream to you.'

'But, Maggie,' replied Iris, with mild astonishment, 'you forget that I am *married* to him. How can I get free, or have the liberty to think of another man? Whilst Mr Harland lives, I must bear my burden as best I can.'

'I don't know that,' said Maggie oracularly. 'He may free you himself, and sooner than you think for, if you'll only leave him alone, and give him enough rope to hang himself with.'

'Maggie! What *do* you mean? Have you heard anything? You see I am afraid even to talk with the other passengers, for fear of my identity becoming known!'

'You talk with Mr Blythe sometimes, and I should think he was a very nice young man to talk with, too,' remarked Maggie dryly.

Iris blushed crimson.

'Oh, yes! he is very kind. I knew

him years ago in Scotland, Maggie. But, of course, I never speak to him of Mr Harland. Indeed, I was so afraid he might find out something about us, that I told him I was a widow, for which I have often been sorry since. But do tell me what you meant by saying that.'

'Well, I meant this, mistress. That that villain (thinking he has got well rid of you and me) is making up to another woman.'

'What woman? Who told you so?' demanded Iris quickly.

'No one told me. I can see it for myself, and all the ship knows it. Though I keep my face well covered when I go on deck, I don't shut my eyes, I can tell you; and there I see him, day after day, and night after night, by the side of the same young lady, whispering in her ear, and goggling at her with those great black eyes of his. So I asked Will their names (just as if it was for curiosity), and he said they was a Mr Harland and a Miss Vansittart; and she's a great heiress, and they are to be married as soon as they get ashore. I said he looked a bad 'un, and I wouldn't trust him with the change for a brass farthing; and then Will told me something about him that— Well, he bound me to secrecy, but all I can say, my pretty, is that the brute's in your power whenever you choose to make use of the knowledge.'

'*In my power*,' repeated Iris dreamily.

She had grown very pale, and clenched her hand as Maggie spoke of her husband's threatened infidelity; for though a woman may have learnt through much tribulation to hate and despise a man, she does not hear with equanimity that he is about to insult and pass her over for another. But as the girl declared that Harland was '*in her power*,' her look of anger changed to one of determination.

'Tell me directly,' she cried, clutching
her arm. 'How is he in my power?
What can I do to revenge myself on
him?'

'Why, mistress, you frighten me!' exclaimed Maggie. 'I never saw you look
like that before. Why should you care
what such a black-hearted villain says or
does, except it be to set you free—'

'Free! Free! What would be the
good of freedom to me, Maggie? Do
you suppose I would ever take advantage of it—to go in bondage to another
man? But Mr Harland shall not marry
this girl. He shall not aggrandise himself at her expense and mine! He shall
not ruin another life, and make another
woman curse the day she ever met him!
No! not if I can prevent it! I have
suffered so deeply—I have wept so much
on account of him, that I feel as if I
could lay down my life to save a fellow-
creature from the same miserable fate!
He shall not marry Miss Vansittart,

Maggie! He shall not even continue to court her, if I can prevent it! But how —*how ?* '

She clasped her head with her hands, and bowed herself over the table.

' Mistress, dear!' cried Maggie. ' My pretty, don't take on! Oh, the brute ain't worth a single tear! If you knew as much as I do, you'd say so too!'

' I *do* say so, and I believe it. Maggie, what shall I do ? '

'Will you speak to Will, my dear? Will you tell him you're that man's wife, and ask his advice? He can give it better than I. And he can tell you something (that I daren't) as will show you that Mr Harland's worse than you ever thought him.'

And here she whispered in her mistress's ear.

' Oh, how dreadful! how awful it all is!' moaned Iris. ' What shall I do ? Who shall I go to ? '

' Why not speak to Mr Blythe, mistress. He's young, but he's your friend; and he's got a head on his shoulders. Tell it all to him.'

'No! no! I can't!' said her companion, shaking her head.

'Well, it's the truth,' replied Maggie, rising to her feet; 'and, if I was you, I'd just leave the brute alone till he's well in the net, and then come down upon him for bigamy. Why, only think of it! You'd be as free as air! And if you stop him, you may be bound all your life.'

'How can I take my happiness at the expense of an innocent person, Maggie?'

'Do you mean Miss Vansittart? I shouldn't call HER innocent! She's just as ready to have him as he is her; and I bet she's never took the trouble to ask if he's married or single. Just like them women! Ready to jump down any man's throat,' said Maggie, with as much indignation as if she had not been a woman herself. 'Well, I'll leave you now, my pretty, and go on deck to have a look after them two, and if I can find out anything more about their doings, I'll come back and let you know.'

'Yes, do go, dear Maggie. I shall be better left alone to think out this new dilemma by myself. Go to your Will, and be as happy as you can; but don't tell him anything about me until we meet again.'

As soon as Maggie met Will Farrell, he saluted her with a fresh story concerning their mutual enemy. A rumour had spread about the ship that Harland had played with marked cards the night before, when he had been particularly lucky at Napoleon; and although there was no verification of the report, it was generally known, and every one was looking askance at him in consequence. Mr Vansittart was especially disturbed. He had taken an unusual fancy for Godfrey Harland, and, notwithstanding his wife's objections to the match, he had encouraged

his attentions to his daughter. Now he
heard with consternation that Mr Fowler
had accused Harland in the smoke-room,
of looking over his neighbour's hand, with
the intent to defraud, and he wished
earnestly that he had been a little more
reticent in his manner towards him. The
accusation was a grave one, but it had
gone no farther at the time, although the
scene that ensued had been very noisy.
But it had not been withdrawn, and Mr
Fowler had refused to tender an apology,
so that the rest of the passengers were
beginning not to see Mr Harland when
he approached them.

'If he ever tries it on again, he'll get
tarred and feathered,' said Farrell, in conclusion.

'And serve him right, too,' replied
Maggie imprudently. 'I know *I'd* like
to have the handling of him—the black
villain!'

'Why, Maggie, what do *you* know
about him?' said Farrell, with surprise.

'Haven't you told me he ruined your life, Will, by palming off his own forgeries upon you?'

'Yes, so he did, and I'll be even with him for it yet. But you spoke as if you had a private grudge against him.'

'And so I have,' whispered the girl, with a sob in her throat. 'Put your head closer, Will, and you shall know all. You know I told you I was a bad girl, and had been ruined by some one who was worse than myself. Well, *that's* the man. Godfrey Harland is my seducer.'

'D—n him!' hissed Farrell, between his teeth; 'it will be another nail in his coffin when we settle our accounts. But how did it happen, my girl? Where did you meet him? Does your mistress know?'

'Ah! no, no!' cried Maggie, as she grasped him convulsively; 'and you must *swear* never to tell her, Will. For I've tried to make it up to her, indeed I have. I knew I wasn't fit to stay by her side, and that if she guessed how bad I was, she'd have sent me away. But she wanted my help and my protection : that was all I stayed for. I couldn't bear to leave her in his clutches—so bad and cruel as he is, and so I tried to forget it all, for her sake. But I hate him all the worse that he should have tempted me to injure such a sweet, dear creature as she is, and as pure as the stars that are shining over us now.'

' But I don't understand you, Maggie. How can that blackguard's behaviour to you injure Miss Douglas ? She doesn't know him, too, does she ? '

' Why, she's *his wife !* There, now, I've let the cat out of the bag ; but you'll keep it sacred, won't you, Will, for my sake, and the dear mistress, for she don't want it known just yet ? '

' *His wife !* ' repeated Farrell. ' Why, I had no idea that he was married. Poor lady ! I *do* pity her. I'd pity a dog that was in his power. But how, then, can he marry Miss Vansittart ? What new devilry is he up to ? Maggie, you and I must prevent this. We have him in our power.'

'Yes, yes ; but we must do nothing until we know it's for the best. Don't you see, Will, that this is why the mistress and I have been hiding all the voyage ? We've been afraid of *his* seeing us ; and except he holds his head too high for the second cabin, he must have done so before this.'

'He's got another reason for not caring for the company of the second cabin, Maggie,' said Farrell, laughing. 'He knows *I'm* there. I met him before we came aboard, and warned him to keep out of my way. But when we get on shore, we'll cry quits. Don't be in a hurry, girl. Bide your time, and you'll see the finest shindy that's ever met your eyes, as soon as we get on shore.'

CHAPTER IX.

THE WHALER.

IT was an intensely cold morning. As the sun raised his golden head of light above the horizon, huge icebergs could be seen far away to the southward, looking like monuments of dazzling crystal'; and a westerly wind, combined with the smell of the bergs, was sufficient to nip any prominent part of the face left exposed to its freezing blast. On board the *Pandora* not a sound was to be heard, save the footsteps of Mr Coffin, as he tramped steadily up and down the deck, turning an occasional glance upon the *Daisy*, a little barque of four hundred tons, that was sailing alongside of them. The *Daisy* was a whaler, built at Glasgow, and hailing from Peterhead. Her commander, Captain Rae, was a rough, weather-beaten old son of Neptune— stern on duty and fearless of danger ; but when on shore (which was seldom), a favourite with women, and beloved of little children. Everybody in Peterhead knew Captain Rae, and accorded him a hearty welcome whenever his barque anchored in port. The men met him with outstretched hands ; the women smiled upon him graciously ; and the children clung to his sleeves and coat tails, like barnacles on a water-logged plank.

'It won't do to go any further down south,' he observed to his chief officer, Mr Green, who had just emerged from the booby hatch, after taking a cup of steaming coffee, 'because we shall be falling in with too much ice, and I like

to give them bergs a wide berth. Besides, I've a notion we shall fall in with
some fish before long, if that darned
passenger packet to leeward don't scare
'em away. Let her come to two points,'
he called out to the man at the wheel.
' Keep her due east.'

And the sailor, having put his helm
down, the captain retired to the sanctity
of his cabin. The mate watched him
disappear, and then, unceremoniously
squirting a jet of tobacco juice on the
unholystoned deck, muttered something
about 'the *Pandora's* petticoats,' and
commenced to take rapid strides along
the boards. Jabez Aminadab Green
was a down-easter—a tall, lanky fellow,
with long body and spindle-shank legs.
He was some years older than the
skipper—streaks of grey having already
shown themselves in his short grey
beard. His eyes were blue, like blue
glass beads, having no expression in
them. He had hollow cheeks, an

aquiline nose, and a wide mouth, which
was generally kept open to display an
irregular set of teeth, stained and de-
cayed by the constant use of tobacco.

At four bells all hands on watch
aboard of both crafts turned to—the
sailors of the *Pandora* being employed
in scrubbing their decks for the recep-
tion of the passengers, whilst the hardy
old whalers lazily crawled out of their
forecastle, and, after dashing a few
buckets of water over the captain's
quarters, betook themselves to the
'tween decks, where they stretched
new lines, and vied with each other in
telling the 'longest twister' (that is,
in nautical parlance, the most improbable
untruth) they could possibly think of.
When the bells were struck to an-
nounce breakfast aboard the *Daisy*,
their sound re-echoed on the *Pandora*,
and the seamen of the . smaller craft
were surprised to see the poop-deck
of their big neighbour crowded with

bright dresses and brighter faces ; whilst the ladies of the *Pandora* wondered, in their turn, at the appearance of so large a crew on such a little vessel, and their interest continued throughout the day.

' *There she spouts!* ' sang out the man on the look-out at the fore-topmast head of the whaler, not half-an-hour afterwards.

' Where away ? ' bawled Mr Green.

' Two points on the starboard bow,' was the answer.

' Aye! aye!' said the mate, catching sight of the whale, as it rose close to the *Pandora.*

' Are there many ? ' hastily inquired Captain Rae, who had deserted his breakfast as soon as he heard the welcome news.

' Wal, I guess so, sir,' replied Mr Green. ' There are some in the wake of that packet ahead theer; and I saw one critter breach away here on the quarter. There he goes again!' continued the mate, pointing to a large dark object which had leapt right out of the water, and fallen in again with a tremendous splash.

When the intelligence reached the saloon of the *Pandora* that a school of whales was playing right under her bow, the passengers, frantic with excitement, left their breakfast to take care of itself, and, gathering together every spy-glass and binocular that could be borrowed or stolen, rushed upon deck, and remained there until the play was over, and the curtain fell.

The *Daisy's* helm was put down, and her foresail laid to the mast, and when her clew garnets were chock-a-block, the boats were quickly but cautiously lowered. The chief officer, in charge of the first boat, was stationed in the stern, grasping a long sweep to steer her with. Six hands on the thwarts manned the oars, and Christopher Thommasen, a Norwegian harpooner, with his deadly weapons, sat in the bow. With long muffled strokes the rowers laid back on their blades, and in a short space of time reached the desired spot, not, however, before they had 'gallied' (or alarmed) one of the 'bulls,' who began to shoot his spout of water to a great height. Some of the 'cows' approached very close to the boat—so close, indeed, that at times she was in imminent danger of being upset, and all hands expected to be toppled into the water, and delivered over to the mercy of Davy Jones.

When the old Norwegian, Christopher Thommasen, had selected his fish, and the boat was pulled in its wake, the order was given, '*Stand up and give it him !*' and the harpooner, poising his dart above his head, and taking careful aim, let the shaft fly with all his might, and it whizzed through the air, embedding itself deeply in the body of the whale.

The wounded creature 'bobtailed,' lashing the billows with its powerful tail, and sending up quantities of white foam, which fell in a heavy shower over the men, drenching them to the skin.

'*Stern all !*' shouted the mate, perceiving their danger, and the frail craft was instantly back-watered out of harm's way. Finding that this manœuvre did not dispose of his assailants, nor relieve him of the agonising harpoon (which he probably mistook for the teeth of a swordfish), the monster of the deep dived to an immense depth, drawing out the line with amazing velocity. This is the whale's method of freeing himself from his piscatorial enemies, who, being unable (as he is) to sustain the pressure of a deep ocean, are compelled to let go of him.

'There goes flukes,' shouted Thommassen, as he saw the whale disappear, and the men shipped their oars, and prepared for an exciting chase. Away went the 'schoolmaster' at his topmost speed, rising at intervals to the surface to give vent to a plaintive moan, and diving again with breathless rapidity, as he towed his persecutors through the water after him at a considerable rate. Then more darts were planted into the heaving flanks of the labouring fish, who had commenced to tremble violently. Red columns of blood spurted from his wounds, and fell back upon his aching sides, dyeing the water around him crimson. Suddenly the 'flurry' (which is the whaling term for the expiring struggles of the fish), and the sharp, cracking noise which had sounded from the blowholes, ceased, and the huge brute turned upwards, and lay upon the ocean dead. Then the carcase was slowly towed past the passenger vessel, amidst the cheers of the spectators, back to the *Daisy,* who had got under weigh again, and made fast to her side by chains. Two men cut off the ' blanket,' or scarf-skin, with their spades, whilst others heaved away on the capstan, and turned the body round.

The head was taken aboard whole, and

then the operation of ' flewsing,' or cutting away the blubber, was gone through. When all the useful parts had been secured —the head, which contains a large amount of oil—the blubber—the bag, from which the whalers extract ambergris, and the teeth—the order was given to ' *Haul in chains*,' and the huge white carcase floated astern, and was immediately covered by myriads of water-fowl, who quarrelled and fought over their unexpected treat.

The passengers of the *Pandora* witnessed the chase and capture from the port bow of their vessel, and many were their ignorant conjectures as to the mode of boiling down and preserving the dead fish, and they watched the *Daisy* perseveringly with their glasses until a large cloud of black smoke, arising from her cauldrons, announced that the blubber had been finally disposed of; and the operation of ' whaling' was over.

CHAPTER X.

DANGER.

BOUT the same time a small wreath of blue smoke was observed issuing from one of the starboard ports of the *Pandora's* half-round, and the alarmed steward rushed upon the quarter-deck, with the terrible news that the ship was on fire. Vernon Blythe was the officer to receive it.

'Unbatten the main hatch,' he shouted, in a loud, clear collected voice to the carpenter, 'and pass out the kegs of gunpowder. Now, lads!' he continued, addressing some of his watch, 'screw on your hose, and lead it through the skylight.'

As the women became alive to the possible danger of their position, they made confusion worse confounded by their screams.

'Jack,' cried Alice Leyton, as she flew to him for protection, 'where shall we go? What shall we do? We shall all be burned to death.'

'Stay where you are, dear,' he answered, hastily but kindly, 'and do nothing. It will all be right in a few minutes. Where is Lovell? Go and stay by him till I tell you all is safe,' and with a nod and a smile he was off to the scene of action.

Alice rushed to her mother, who was half-fainting in a wicker chair, and flung herself at her feet.

'Oh, he was too good for me. I was a fool not to see it. If anything happens to him, I shall never forgive myself,' she said incoherently, as she began to weep with fear.

Mrs Vansittart was leaning on her
husband's arm, pale with fright, as she
begged him to say if she had ever failed
in her duty to him during the last twenty
years ; her daughter Grace was trying to
extract some consolation from Godfrey
Harland, who appeared to be more
alarmed than herself, and all the other
passengers were watching the threatened
danger with faces white with suspense
and fear. At the moment of the alarm,
Mr Coffin happened to be between his
blankets, snoring loudly, and Captain
Robarts was in a similar position in his
cabin, but both men were soon awakened
to a sense of what was going on in the
vessel.

Jack Blythe, having given a few in-
structions to the crew, rushed down the
narrow passage to the saloon, and having
ascertained from which berth the smoke
was issuing, he entered it without ceremony. A small box lay upon the floor.
Placing his hand upon the cover, he lifted

it up, but not before the iron bands sur-
rounding it had burned his palm, and as
soon as it was done, the cabin was illu-
mined by a sheet of flame. Tearing off
his coat, Jack threw it on the burning
mass, but was obliged immediately to re-
treat, half blinded and suffocated by the
dense volumes of smoke his garment produced. Pressing forward again with a
large glass decanter of water from the
saloon sideboard, he succeeded in extin-
guishing the flames in the box, but not
before the bed-clothes were all on fire.

By that time he was joined by some of
the others, amongst whom was Captain
Robarts with the hose, which Jack
snatched from him, and played upon the
burning articles, but the cabin was gutted
and the bulkhead charred before the fire
was out and the danger over.

Jack's hair was scorched by the flame,
and his eyes smarting and blackened by
the smoke, as he emerged from the saloon,
and drew in a deep breath of the fresh air.

'Are you hurt, Mr Blythe?' inquired Captain Robarts, who was proud of his smart young officer.

'Not a bit, sir. My hair won't want cutting again just yet,' said Jack, passing his hand over his singed locks; 'and the fire caught my ears a little. But I'm all right, and the ship's all right, which is much more to the purpose.'

'Thanks to your promptitude and courage, sir,' replied the skipper.

The compliment was formal, but Jack coloured with pleasure to receive it, from brow to chin.

'How did the fire originate? Where did it come from? Who put it out? What damage has it done?' were the queries put by the various passengers, whose fears soon calmed down as they were apprised of their safety. But no one could answer them.

'Mr Greenwood, Captain Robarts desires to see you in the saloon,' said the steward, when the bustle and confusion were somewhat abated ; and the young gentleman followed him to the presence of the master of the *Pandora*.

The captain was seated at the table, with his log-book before him.

' I have sent for you, Mr Greenwood,' he commenced, in a stern voice, ' to ask how this fire originated. The smoke and the flames came from your cabin, and I understand you were the last person to leave it. How did it happen ? '

' I'm sure I can't tell you, sir,' replied young Greenwood, who was trembling under the captain's gaze.

' But no one has been in the berth but yourself,' rejoined Captain Robarts ; ' my steward is a witness to that.'

' But I don't think it could have been *me*, sir, don't you know ? ' spluttered the youth, ' because— '

' What were you doing there ? ' thundered the skipper ; ' come, sir, no nonsense with me. The lives of the whole ship's company have been endangered, and I *will* find out the cause. What did you come down for? Tell me at once. As captain of this vessel, I have a right to question you.'

Harold Greenwood had heard of other rights possessed by the captain of a vessel, such as putting mutinous subjects under arrest, and fearful of what the consequences of telling an untruth might be, he stammered out that he only came down to fetch a cigarette.

'And where did you light your cigarette, Mr Greenwood?' continued the captain relentlessly.

'In the berth,' blurted out the young man, 'but I threw the match into the basin, don't you know? I am *sure* I did. I always do; and that can't do any harm, eh?'

'Steward, go with Mr Greenwood, and get the lucifer out of the basin,' said the skipper; and whilst Harold tremblingly followed the servant, the captain leaned his head upon his hand,

and seemed lost in thought. The search was unsuccessful. No trace of a burnt lucifer could be found in the basin.

'But I'm *sure* I did,' stammered Greenwood.

'*I* will tell you what you did, Mr Greenwood,' interrupted the captain angrily. 'You lighted your cigarette, and dropped the still burning match into the box, and set fire to my vessel. You are well aware that smoking is prohibited in the saloon, yet by your disobedience and carelessness you have endangered the lives of my passengers and crew. Had it not been for the presence of mind of my second officer, the whole ship would have been blown out of the water.'

'I'm sure, sir, I'm very sorry, don't you know?'

'*Sorry*, sir! what use would your being sorry have been when we were all dead men? You're a fool, sir, that's what you are—a d—d fool! You can leave me now. I shall enter the facts as they occurred, into

my official log, and you will be charged
with the damages, and I only hope your
father may stop your allowance in consequence, and leave you less money to waste
on cigarettes and matches, for the future.
I have nothing further to say to you, sir,
and you can go.'

Harold Greenwood sneaked out of the
austere presence, looking very small and
pitiful, and found to his horror, on reach-
ing the deck, that the whole conversation
had been overheard by the inquisitive
passengers, who had listened attentively
to it through the skylight. And he had
the further mortification of hearing Jack
Blythe's cool-headed pluck lauded on all
sides, by the same tongues that reproached
him for his stupidity and want of care.

'Allow me to congratulate you, Blythe,'
said Captain Lovell, 'you possess all the
attributes of a hero.'

'We owe you a vote of thanks,' added
Mr Vansittart. 'Had it not been for
your courage, sir, we might all have been

blown to smithereens by this time, and our limbs scattered to the four quarters of the globe.'

'But you've lost your coat, I hear,' said Miss Vere; 'we must get you the very best that's made, by general subscription, Mr Blythe.'

'And, oh, Jack, you've hurt your hand!' cried Alice Leyton plaintively, 'and your hair is burnt right off to the roots, in front. Won't you do anything for yourself, when you have done so much for us?'

'Belay that, Alice,' replied the young sailor laughingly. 'You know how I hate fuss of all sort. And as for my hand, it is only a little scorched, and will be all right to-morrow. I've had it twice as sore after handling the ropes, I can tell you.'

'Ah, you never *would* let any one thank you, whatever you did for them,' said Alice, with a sigh.

But there she made a mistake. There were *some* thanks that Vernon Blythe accepted greedily, and treasured the remem-

brance of in his heart of hearts. As the
night fell, and he sought out Iris Harland
on the quarter-deck, her hand grasped his
with a feverish pressure.

'We have heard it *all*,' she said, with
a warm, grateful light in the eyes she
bent on him ; ' Maggie and I were in the
cabin when the alarm broke out, and at
first I was very much frightened. But
the steward or some one called out that it
was Mr Blythe's watch, and he had gone
to see what it was all about. And then
somehow, I felt quite satisfied. It seemed
as if it *must* be all right, if *you* were there.'

' Is that *really* the case, Iris ? Was the
sense of my presence and protection such
a comfort to you as all that ? '

' Indeed it was. I have only told you
the truth. You are so brave and strong,
and you seem so fearless yourself, that
you inspire others with courage.'

' It makes me very happy to hear you
say so. Yet I was not quite so fearless
as you give me credit for, Iris. When I

first perceived the possibility of danger,
the thought of *one* person on board this
vessel came into my mind, and almost
paralysed me, until the same thought
nerved my arm, and made me feel as if I
could dare and do anything for her sake.'

'That was the young lady you are engaged to, Mr Blythe, I suppose. You
see, we hear all the chatter in the second
cabin. Maggie has pointed her out to
me—Miss Leyton, I mean—and I think
she is very pretty. And, Mr Blythe,'
continued Iris, in a sweet, faltering voice,
'I *do* hope you will be happy with her. I
—I—don't think marriage is a very happy
condition myself, but there are always ex-
ceptions, and I shall pray yours may be
one of them.'

'I think it will, if it ever comes to pass.
But that will not be with Alice Leyton,
Iris. Maggie and you are both mistaken.
I am not engaged to her, or any woman.
In fact, I believe she is on the point of
being engaged to Captain Lovell.

'Indeed! Then it was not *she* who inspired your deed of daring?'

'No. Quite another person. But you must not speak of a common act of duty by such an absurd name. There was never any positive danger. A young fool called Greenwood lit his cigar in the berth, and dropped the burning lucifer, which set the whole cabin in a blaze. Of course, it *might* have resulted in a disaster. But it won't do in this life to calculate on our "might-have-beens," unless we wish to turn it into a book of Lamentations.'

'Have you missed so many chances, then, Mr Blythe? I should not have thought so.'

'I have missed *one*, Iris, for which no future success can ever repay me. Cannot you guess what that was?'

'You don't mean that old business at the Bridge of Allan, surely?' she said, in a low voice.

'Indeed I do. I do not blame *you* for

one moment, remember. I know that it was not your fault, and that I alone was to blame for my presumption in daring to love you, but it has spoilt my life.'

They were standing by the side of the vessel looking into the rushing sea as he spoke to her, and they were almost alone. The evening was so cold that none of the saloon passengers were on the poop, and the quarter-deck was nearly deserted. Maggie sat in a sheltered corner under the long-boat, by the side of Will Farrell, but they were too far off, and too much engrossed by each other, to hear what their companions said. And so Iris, wrapped in a dark cloak, stood, under the cover of night, with her sad eyes up-raised, and her pure profile limned against the evening sky; and Vernon Blythe lingered by her side, looking with infinite love and yearning on her face. He was dreaming all sorts of wild, impossible dreams as he did so, but the wakening was coming to him only too soon.

'*It has spoilt your life,*' repeated Iris, in a tone of incredulity. 'Oh, don't say that, Mr Blythe. You make me feel so very miserable and guilty.'

' Have I not just said that I acquit you of any intentional unkindness ? How could you have been expected to believe that such a lad as I was should presume to lift his eyes to you ? But, you see, I couldn't help it. It was a sort of fate with me. I saw you and loved you from the beginning, and since then I have tried to put you out of my mind by every possible means, in vain. You *will* stick there. You are so obstinate.'

Iris laughed faintly.

'I am very, *very* sorry. I must seem like an obstinate Irish tenant to you, who pays no rent, and yet refuses to turn out. Why don't you evict me ? '

'I wouldn't evict you if I could,' said the young man warmly.

'I don't think,' went on Iris dreamily, that I quite knew what I was about in those days, Mr Blythe. I was only eighteen, you know (I am twenty-three now), and I had lived all my life in the country with my father, and he never looked after me, or advised me, as my mother would have done. If my poor mother had lived, I don't think I should ever have married—as I did marry. But I was so ignorant. I knew nothing.'

'Iris,' said Vernon suddenly, 'tell me all about your marriage. I never heard more than the mere facts. I don't even know your married name, unless it was "Douglas." But why do you call yourself "*Miss?*" Why are you going out to Dunedin? What was your husband, and when did he die? Would it be painful for you to tell me all this?'

'Very painful. Please don't ask me. My past life is like a bad dream to me.'

'Then you were not happy with him?'

'No.'

'Did he dare to ill-treat you?' exclaimed Vernon.

Iris was silent.

'My God!' cried the young man fiercely; 'were he only on earth, he should answer to me for this.'

'Hush! hush! Mr Blythe. Let us drop the subject. It is all over now,' said Iris trembling.

'But *is* it all over? Can any future life (however happy) give you back your peace of mind, your lovely, girlish innocence, your health and strength? I parted with you rich in every gift that youth and hope can give—able and willing to speak of yourself, your past and your future; I meet you again, broken in health and spirits, with dark passages in your life which you dare not speak of— with no prospects, and no friends. Iris, it is killing me! I was a boy then, it is true, without future, or experience, or anything to recommend me in your eyes. But I *loved* you, passionately and devotedly, and even though you did not love me, I could have made you happier

than this.   Oh, why did you throw yourself away on a man who could not appreciate you ? '

'How can I answer a question to you
which I cannot answer to myself.   I
suppose I was mad, or blind.   He was
good-looking, and an adept at deception,
and I was too inexperienced to distin-
guish the true metal from the false.
Don't blame me for it too much, Mr
Blythe.   I liked you very much.   I felt
honoured by your preference, and I have
never forgotten it since.   But you seemed
such a boy to me then, and I did not
know—I could not tell—' she faltered,
breaking down.

'But I am not a boy now,' urged
Vernon eagerly ; 'I was twenty-five last
birthday.   You will not accuse me again
of not knowing my own mind.   Oh, Iris,
I have never ceased to love, and dream
of you.   In my lonely watches, in tem-
pests and in calm — from the torrid to
the frigid zone—it has been all the same.

Your dear image, the echo of your voice, the crumbs of comfort you threw to me in my distress, have been hugged to my heart as its best treasures. And it will be so till I die, even should I live for another half century.'

'What am I to say to you?' she answered, weeping, 'except that it can never, *never* be. Oh, Mr Blythe, don't talk to me of love. It is useless! It can end in nothing! I—I—must not listen to you.

'But *why?* What is the obstacle? Do you love any one else?'

Iris shook her head.

'And do you dislike me?'

She did not shake her head this time, but she looked up at the sky, and he could see the large tears that stood in her eyes, course slowly down her cheeks.

'Oh, my darling!' he exclaimed rapturously, as he threw his arms around her, 'I have conquered at last. You need not trouble yourself to give me any other answer.'

But Iris twisted herself out of his embrace, and turned her pale face towards him.

'Don't! Pray, pray, don't!' she said earnestly. 'I—I—cannot bear it! I appreciate all you have said to me at its full value, and I shall never forget it. But there it must end! For I have deceived you, Mr Blythe! I am not a widow! I—I—am *still married.*'

As this announcement left her lips, Vernon Blythe felt as if he had been struck right across the face. He turned as white as a sheet, looked her fixedly in the eyes for a moment, then dropping her hand, he turned on his heel, and walked silently away.

CHAPTER XI.

SHIPPING SEAS.

 STRONG westerly wind coursed the Southern ocean, and gigantic green waves rolled on all sides of the *Pandora*, sometimes rushing up against her with pugilistic violence, and depositing tons of water on her deck. White clouds drifted across the heavens with tremendous speed, upon a background of cerulean blue. A grey bank, however, that stretched from aft to the starboard beam, betokened the advent of hail, or snow, whilst the sun

struggled at times to pour his feeble rays upon the surface of the deep.

The *Pandora* was running before the gale.   Her mainsails and crossjack were stowed, to permit the foresail to have full play, which bellied out to such an extent that it pressed tightly against the sheep-skin chafing-gear on the forestay.   The fore-topmast staysail and inner jib, flapping idly to and fro, might have had the gaskets round them, for all the good that they were doing, and the smaller sails on the mizen were furled, to keep the main royal and top-gallant sail full, lest she should take in too much water aft.

The heavy swells made the ship roll violently, often dipping her main bumpkins into the water, and agitating the compass card to such an extent that the man at the wheel could not depend on its accuracy, for ascertaining the true position of the vessel's head.

At mid-day the sun had risen behind a squall, and Captain Robarts, after waiting patiently for twenty minutes, with sextant in hand, carried his instrument below again, and went to luncheon, not, however, without a growl at the obstructing cloud which prevented his getting the meridian altitude.

The hour for lunch was gladly welcomed by the passengers that day, for their appetites had been sharpened by the keen wind, and punctual to the moment, all were seated in their accustomed places.

Vernon Blythe, arrayed in his long silk oilskin coat and 'sou'-wester,' having relieved Mr Coffin, was in charge of the vessel, and the watch were huddled together round the mainmast, standing by to take his orders.

As the sky became darker with the squall, large flakes of snow fell upon the deck, and increased in number, until the *Pandora* was enveloped in a blinding sheet of white.

'It is useless to look at the compass,'

said Vernon Blythe, as he watched the helmsman trying to clear the face with his mitten. 'Watch her head, man, and give her as few spokes as possible.'

The *Pandora's* steering-gear was of the latest invention, and a reliable quartermaster would have found no difficulty in guiding her on her course. But the man at the helm had been taught to steer by the compass only, and when the snow covered the glass of the binnacle and obscured the points, he was utterly at a loss how to proceed, and quite unfit, in consequence, for the responsible post he held.

When, therefore, the ship ran off her course, he gave her so many spokes that she came flying to—the weather leeches shivered, the headsails filled, and she shipped an enormous sea, which thumped upon the deck right amidships, and ran in a boisterous torrent forward.

Vernon Blythe saw the ship's mad caperings, and shouted to the helmsman

to put his helm up, before she was broad-
side on. But he was too late. The
mischief was done. With the backward
roll of the *Pandora*, as she lifted over the
swells, the mighty stream of water flowed
aft. The steward, unprepared for such a
disaster, had not shipped the weather
board, and the sea poured through the
cabin passage, taking him clean off his
legs, and drenching both himself and a
roast turkey, which he was about pomp-
ously to place on the saloon table, with
salt water.

The sailors at the main, knowing what
to expect when scudding with such a sea,
jumped on the fiferail, and clung to the
crossjack braces, thus saving themselves
a ducking.

But the assault was not yet over. Immediately succeeding the first sea, a
second cataract of water leapt over at
the main chains, and doubled the large
amount which was already aboard. At
this disaster, dismay and confusion reigned

paramount in the saloon. Ladies and gentlemen left their luncheon alike, as the latter rushed about to see if they could render any serviceable assistance, and the former, with piteous little shrieks for help, lifted their petticoats, and jumped on the seats, to keep their feet out of the water.

'We are going down!' cried Mrs Vansittart. 'Oh, John, I knew no good would come of our going to England.'

'Mother!' screamed Alice Leyton, 'the sea is filling the ship! Oh, where is Jack?'

'Don't leave me, Godfrey,' murmured Grace Vansittart, as she clung to her lover's shoulders.

'Ladies, I beg of you not to be alarmed. I can assure you there is not the slightest danger,' commenced Captain Robarts; but an accident, which had its comical as well as its serious side, prevented the conclusion of his sentence. The benches on which the party had been seated were made of oak, with broad backs, fastened to the deck on either side with brass screws. Consequently, when the ladies scrambled on them, and stood as far back as they possibly could, with their skirts gathered in their hands, the whole of their weight was thrown on the supports. The oaken benches were strong, but the fastenings were not, and the unusual strain drew the screws from their hold, and caused the entire structure to give way. With piercing screams and exclamations, clutching at the fiddles and the tablecloths, and dragging the china and glass on the top of them, the men and women were precipitated backwards into the stream of water, where they lay in a confused heap, struggling and spluttering, but unable to extricate themselves. Their heads were against the doors and partitions of the private cabins, whilst their bodies rested on the seats of the benches, which were partly underneath them. The deplorable but ridiculous scene can better be imagined than described. Rolls, pats

of butter, cold chickens, potatoes, and
empty bottles of beer were floating about
the cabin floor, whilst the dish-covers and
glasses were mostly in their laps, or
surging against their faces.   The men
could not move, any more than their fair
companions, and whilst some swore and
others sobbed with fright and humiliation,
the cold salt water kept 'swishing' over
them all.

Captain Robarts, from his arm-chair of
state, viewed the accident as an every-
day occurrence, and awaited its termina-
tion with complacency, not offering the
slightest assistance to any one.   But Mr
Coffin, with his mouth full of roast goose,
and a wicked smile of amusement on his
face, gallantly went to the rescue.   Mrs
Vansittart was the first saved from the
deluge, with the colour considerably less-
ened in her honest, rosy face.   Captain
Lovell was next hauled out, but he made
light of the affair, and burst into a loud
laugh, which was instantly stopped by

the aggrieved and indignant looks of Alice Leyton.

'How can you laugh in that unfeeling way,' she said, 'when I feel bruised all over? But of course you're not hurt yourself, and so it does not signify. Men are the most selfish creatures in the world.'

'By Jove! it's spoilt my new suit, though, don't you know?' observed Mr Greenwood, looking the picture of misery, as he examined the state of his garments.

'You did your best to burn us out of house and home the other day, Mr Greenwood,' said the captain grimly, 'so you mustn't be surprised if no one sympathises with you over a ducking.'

'*We* shall be none the worse for it,' remarked Mr Fowler, shaking himself like a huge water-dog; 'it's the ladies who are to be pitied for wetting their pretty dresses, and prettier faces.'

But the women did not wait to be

condoled with. As soon as they had regained a normal position, and ascertained there was nothing to be frightened at in 'shipping a sea,' they ran away to their berths to change their clothes, and recover the shock sustained by their modesty.

In the second cabin the passengers had not escaped a wetting. Plenty of water had penetrated the hatch, and made their abode damp and uncomfortable, and it was not until the first dog-watch had commenced, and the swinging lamps were lit, that they could sit with dry feet in the general dining-room.

'My pretty,' whispered Maggie Greet, as she crept up to Iris's side for a moment, 'you'll have to keep to your berth this evening, if you don't want to have a shindy, for Will says as *he's* coming down to play here with the others.'

'*Mr Harland?*' exclaimed Iris, blanching like a lily. 'Oh, Maggie! *why* does he come here? Who asked him?'

'I don't know, dear. Not Mr Farrell, you may be sure, for they hate each other like poison. But Will says he's been kicked out of every other cabin. They're fighting very shy of him up-stairs, as well they may. And he over-heard a gentleman asking Mr Harland why he didn't come down and play on the lower deck, and he said he'd try it to-night. So be on your guard, that's all.'

'What shall I do?' said Iris distress-fully. 'If he takes to it as a custom, he will drive me to take refuge in my berth every evening. I never thought the saloon passengers would be allowed down here.'

'Well! I expect, if you want to get rid of him, you've only to show yourself. I believe he'd rather see the devil just now than you. For *he* don't interfere with his wickedness, but *you* will! It would be all up with his game with Miss Vansittart, if you told your true name to the captain! Wouldn't it, my dear?'

'And that is what I shall be compelled to do, Maggie, sooner or later. I cannot stand by and see him commit such a wickedness, and hold myself guiltless.'

'Not even if you could have Mr— I mean a better man instead of him,' insinuated Maggie.

'No, Maggie! a better man wouldn't take me on such conditions. But I don't want to shame Mr Harland before all the ship, if a more private means of warning him will have the same effect. I sit sometimes for hours and try to decide what will be for the best, and I always come to the same conclusion— that I am one of the most unfortunate women on the face of the earth.'

'Never mind, my pretty,' whispered Maggie consolingly, 'it'll all come right some day. I have doubts about myself sometimes, because I've been a wicked girl, and it don't seem right as I *should* be happy. But I've none about you! I can see it as plain as a picture, and if I don't live to see it, it will be all the same. You'll have a good man and a true, please God, some day, to make up to you for the past!'

And Maggie turned away with a sob.

'Why, dear Maggie! what's the matter with you to-night?'

'Nothing, mistress, only Will's too good to me sometimes, and makes me so ashamed of myself. But there now, the gentlemen are beginning to come down for their game, so I must run away, and you'd better do the same.'

And so the two women, who owed much of their immunity from discovery to Will Farrell's careful look out on their behalf, kissed each other, and separated for the night.'

The origin of this conversation was, that since the breaking up of the card-parties in the smoke-room, owing to the loose play of Godfrey Harland, the deck-house had been deserted of an evening, and the gentlemen had betaken themselves elsewhere.

Some played in the spacious berth of the second officers, others preferred the society of the ladies, and a few were invited to the second cabin, where smoking was not prohibited, and their less aristocratic fellow-passengers did their utmost to make them feel at home.

Many a game at dominoes or whist had been played there lately by the men from the saloon, who had become so friendly with its rightful owners that they did not even wait for an invitation. Besides, in many respects, the second cabin was preferable to the deckhouse. In the former the steward was always at hand to provide refreshments, whilst in the latter, if a man wished for anything, he was compelled to go on deck and find the head steward, which interrupted the game, and annoyed all concerned.

Since the cardroom had been closed, Godfrey Harland's time hung heavily upon his hands. He was not quite so bold and open as he had been in paying court to Grace Vansittart. He fancied her father and mother looked somewhat more coolly on him than they had done at first, and preferred whispering ' soft nothings ' to her, when they found themselves alone. So he did not care to be shut up in the state cabin all the evening, where every look he gave, and word he uttered, was seen, heard, and commented upon. He was debarred from entering the berth of Vernon Blythe. An instinctive dislike existed between these two young men, and made itself apparent every time they met. So the only resource left to him seemed the second cabin, to which a young fellow of the name of Pemberton had warmly invited him. Harland knew he should meet Will Farrell there, but on the whole he thought it advisable he should meet and make friends with him before

they parted company.   But he little thought
how much more Farrell knew of him now
than he had done when they last saw each
other.   Had he done so, he would have
known he had better have entered a
cockatrice's den than the second cabin of
the *Pandora.*

CHAPTER XII.

A GAME OF DOMINOES.

'GOOD - EVENING, Mr Harland. You are a stranger here,' said Farrell, as he entered. 'I thought you were going to slight your humble friend (meaning myself) throughout the voyage, but—'

'So you have met before,' interrupted Mr Pemberton, who was of the party.

'Oh, yes, we *have* met before—many years ago,' drawled Harland.

'When we were clerks in the same office,' put in Farrell.

'Quite a boyish acquaintance,' said the

other, with an uneasy laugh, for Farrell's manner had annoyed him.

' Many people say that boyish acquaintances last the longest, and are the least soon forgotten,' remarked Pemberton.

' I don't think Mr Harland and I shall forget each other in a hurry,' laughed Farrell sarcastically. ' The memory of Mr Horace—I mean of the office and all that occurred there, will follow me to my grave!'

' Come, come! Let us get to business!' interposed Pemberton, seeing that the two men were at daggers-drawn with one another, though for what cause was a mystery to him. ' Shall we make up a four at dominoes ? '

' I am agreeable!' returned Farrell.

' And so am I,' said Harland ; ' will the ladies join us ? '

' I am afraid not,' answered Farrell. ' The deck is too wet for them ; but I will ask, if you like.'

To his entreaties at the doors of the

ladies' berths he received nothing but negatives. Miss Douglas was already in bed, Miss Grant was afraid of the damp, and Mrs Medlicott was nursing a sick child. But a volunteer was soon found in the person of Bob Perry.

' What do you play for ? ' inquired Harland, when they had turned up the two highest and lowest, and Farrell and Pemberton had been elected partners. ' What do you say to threepence each on the pips that stand out ? '

' Oh, no ! ' exclaimed Perry, ' that is too much. It may run up to a matter of five shillings a game, and I can't afford it.'

' Well, we can't play for *love*,' sneered Harland ; ' never you mind, Perry, I'll stand bail for both of us.'

' I object to that,' said Farrell. ' I do not wish to play for such high stakes any more than Mr Perry. I am simply playing to make the time pass, and don't want to make or lose money by the game. You forget, Mr Harland, that we are not all like yourself, on a trip *for pleasure !*'

He emphasised the words unpleasantly, and Harland swore under his breath, but answered nothing.

'Suppose we play for threepence a game,' suggested Mr Pemberton. 'As Farrell says, we don't want to make money by the stones. All that is necessary to give zest to the victory is a small stake that shall benefit the winner without breaking his companions.'

'All right,' assented Harland, in anything but a good humour; 'go ahead. Double six begins. But, stop a minute. Before we start, we will toss for drinks round.'

To this proposition the other men were not strong-minded enough to object, and the silver coins were spun in the air, and clinked upon the table, resulting, luckily for them, in Godfrey Harland having to pay the forfeit, and the steward was despatched to the bar with the orders.

The game was finished, and the players tossed again, and the stones · were divided, and so it went on until five bells was struck, which was the signal for all the ship lights to be extinguished.

' Lights out, please!' sung out the third officer at the booby hatch.

' In one minute, Mr Sparkes,' replied Harland. ' Let us finish the game, there's a good fellow.'

' It is against the rule,' said the junior mate ; ' I cannot disobey my orders.'

'Come down and have a glass of whisky, then,' urged Mr Pemberton ; ' we have more than half a bottle left.'

To this invitatation Mr Richard Sparkes did not reply that he could not disobey orders, but glancing aft to satisfy himself that the ' old man ' was not on deck, he quickly descended the companion, and stepping up to the table, muttered his thanks, and swallowed the intoxicating draught.

'You understand, don't you, Sparkes,' said Harland ; 'we sha'n't be a minute, old man. Just shut down the hatch, and cover it with a tarpaulin, and if that d—d inquisitive second mate of yours discovers the glim, I'll take the blame on myself.'

Whereupon, without another word, the third officer left them to their pursuits. When the game had come to a conclusion, Pemberton signified his intention to turn in, and bidding them good-night, went to his cabin. Bob Perry, who was half - seas over, also retired, and the two belligerents were alone together. It was for this that Farrell had taken a hand at the game. It was to this end he had worked to find himself cheek - by - jowl with the man he hated more deadlily than he had ever done before. He thirsted to put a spoke in Harland's wheel,—to alarm him thoroughly,—to show a little of his own hand, but not too much, and make him uncomfortable for the remainder of the voyage.

'Drink up and have some more,' said Harland, breaking the silence that ensued on the departure of their companions.

'I don't care for any. I have had enough,' replied Farrell, lying back in his chair. 'Well, our journey will soon be over now. What do you intend to do when we reach Lyttleton?'

'I don't know, I'm sure,' returned Harland. 'I shall enjoy myself as long as I find anything worth enjoying, and then, perhaps, take a trip over to America, and visit some of my friends there.'

'But I thought you had taken service under Mr Vansittart, and were bound to remain with him?' said Farrell.

Godfrey Harland opened his eyes with astonishment.

'Then you are under a great delusion. I have certainly promised to be the guest of the Vansittarts for a short time, and circumstances may arise to detain me longer, but there is no obligation in the matter, unless it be on *my* side.'

'Oh! indeed. People say otherwise on board. I have heard it stated confidently that you are Mr Vansittart's land-agent, and that he has been imprudent enough to take you without references.'

' D—n their impertinence!' growled Harland, 'prying into other people's affairs. I should like to know the name of the person who has been spreading these false reports about me.'

'*I* shall not tell you,' retorted Farrell. ' It is quite immaterial to me whether you keep Mr Vansittart, or Mr Vansittart keeps you, but I should think the latter by far the most probable of the two. And is it true that you intend to marry his daughter ? '

' It is no business of yours if I do.'

'Certainly not. It's no business of mine if you turn Mormon, which, I suppose, is the next thing you'll think of.'

'What do you mean by making that remark ?' said Harland, turning pale.

'Only that English laws are in force in the colonies, and a man is only allowed to have one wife at a time.'

'What would you insinuate, you scoundrel ?' demanded Harland, beginning to feel alarmed.

'Softly — softly,' said Will Farrell, 'don't raise your voice. Some one might overhear you. I never insinuate, as I think I informed you at our last meeting ; I always speak my mind, and if you wish me to do so now, I will. I will go further, and take our fellow-passengers into my confidence, if you desire to become notorious amongst them.'

'What would you tell them ?' demanded Harland, livid with passion.

'That you have a wife already, and cannot marry Miss Vansittart.'

'It is a lie! I was never married to her.'

Farrell was staggered for a moment by

this bold assertion. What if it were true. The man before him was villain enough for anything, and the first thing a woman tries to hide is her own shame. Yet Maggie had said that Iris was his wife, and he did not believe that Maggie would tell an untruth.

'That is easily settled,' he answered quickly; 'we can appeal to Mrs Harland.'

'You cannot. She is dead.'

'That is a lie!' cried Farrell fiercely, 'as great a lie as the other. I *know* your wife to be alive.'

'Where have you seen her?'

'I shall not tell you.'

'I will *make* you!' exclaimed Harland, advancing upon him.

But Farrell was prepared for the attack.

'Dare to lay a finger on me,' he said, 'and the whole ship shall hear your story.'

'What story have you to tell them?' repeated his adversary.

'One that would make two or three columns of the most interesting reading in the daily papers, Mr Horace Cain. Only a little incident that occurred a few years since (how many was it—*ten?*) at Starling's Bank. A forged cheque—the warrant for an arrest—a fruitless search —an escape to America — and what *I* should call a most imprudent return. I should point out the hero of the piece to them—it would be quite a melodrama. Virtue triumphant, vice in the background, and the blue fire of their indignation over all.'

'And who would believe your story?' sneered Harland.

'I would *make* them believe it,' resumed Farrell, in a sadder and more earnest voice. 'I would point to myself as its best proof,—to *me* whom your bad example ruined — whom your cowardice left in the lurch—on whom the stigma of your villainy fell like a curse, rising up like the deadly nightshade to poison every

home I tried to make for myself. Godfrey Harland (as you choose to call yourself), you have been my bad genius from
the day we met. You tempted me to evil,
and left me to bear the brunt of your
own misdemeanonr. You have ruined
others beside myself—(I know more of
your doings than you think of). But
your day is ended. Before you blight
another life, as you have done mine, I
will blazon the miserable truth to the
world.'

'Where would your proofs be?' cried
Harland; 'and who would credit your
simple word. I'd soon hash your goose
for you, my fine fellow. A low second-
class passenger attempting to blackguard
a gentleman! I'd tell them you had tried
to extort money from me, and failed, and
they would accept my statement much
sooner than yours; and in all probability
you would receive an injunction from the
captain to keep the peace, or be put
under arrest. Why, you're not sober

now, you useless, drunken " ne'er-do-
weel." Don't you presume on your former knowledge to speak to me again. I
have done with you from this moment.'

And Harland rose to leave the spot.

'And don't you dare to venture down
here again,' replied Farrell, trembling with
excitement, 'or I will carry out my threat,
and expose you before the whole ship's
company, as Mr Horace Cain, the for—'

'Take care what you say,' interrupted
Harland, in a hoarse voice, 'or I shall
not be able to control my temper. I have
stood your insults long enough.'

'Not longer than I have submitted to
yours. And I have a double debt to
discharge to you now, Mr Harland.
You think that I know nothing,—that I
am powerless to damage your character.
What about Maggie Greet, who served
your deserted wife in England?'

At that name, Godfrey Harland felt his
limbs tremble. The thought of Maggie
Greet had always had more power to sting

his hardened conscience than that of his wife. He was more afraid of her than of Iris, and less certain of her keeping his secrets.

'I don't know to whom you allude,' he replied, attempting to brave it out. 'Was she the "slavey?" You really cannot expect me to remember the names of those sort of people.'

'And yet she remembers *you*,' said Farrell sarcastically. 'How strange. And she remembers the wrong you did her into the bargain. Stranger still, isn't it?'

'Oh, enough of this cursed twaddle!' cried Harland, who was most anxious to get away. 'You are talking of a lot of things of which you know nothing. I am off to bed now. Let us thoroughly understand each other. If you presume to speak to me again, I shall cut you dead.'

'And if you come down to the second cabin again, I'll break every bone in your body,' retorted Farrell. 'And when I get you on shore, my boy, we'll have it out, whoever is by to see, and let the best man win.'

Harland was on the top rung of the ladder, and as he heard Will Farrell's parting threat he turned pale with fear, and the beads of perspiration stood on his forehead like dew.

What if any one should have overheard his words. He pushed up the hatch, and alighting on the deck, staggered to his cabin, and threw himself upon the berth in a state bordering on despair.

CHAPTER XIII.

IN THE SMOKE-ROOM.

THE accident that occurred to little Winifred Leyton, and the rough weather that succeeded it, had pretty well driven the idea of the proposed theatricals out of the ladies' heads. In the first place, an unaccountable gloom seemed to have fallen upon the amateur company, and they became so indifferent about the whole affair, that Miss Vere left them to themselves, and sought refuge in her own studies.

Alice Leyton and Captain Lovell looked as if the world were over for both of them.

He had been afraid, since his interview with Mrs Leyton, to speak more openly to her daughter than he had done, and the girl imagined, in consequence, that he had been trifling with her. She spent her time, therefore, in gazing in a melancholy fashion over the sea, whilst he sat at the opposite side of the deck and gazed at her ; and Miss Vere said she was quite sick of them both.

Jack Blythe, too, was not in his usual spirits. The fair manageress had fully intended to enlist the handsome young officer amongst her volunteers, but he had decidedly refused to take any part in the amusement, and she laid it all down to the charge of Alice Leyton, and grew still more angry with her in consequence. But when the cold weather continued to debar the ladies from sitting on deck, and the evenings became long and tedious, the idea of the theatricals was once more revived, and hailed as a distraction. Since the smoke-room had been deserted by the card-players, the younger couples had crept in and taken possession of it, and on the morning after the swamping of the after cabin, several of them assembled there, with their books and work and writing, Captain Lovell, as usual, looking unutterable things at the love-stricken Alice, and Mr Fowler, who had never disclosed the secrets of his past, his present, nor his future, to his fellow-passengers, basking in the smiles of Miss Vere, with whom he was a great favourite. Poor Harold Greenwood, who had fallen into terrible disgrace with most of the ship's company since his little *escapade* with the lighted lucifer, and who had tried to indemnify himself for cold looks and flagging conversation, by falling hopelessly in love with the actress, was worshipping her at a respectful distance, and Pemberton was doing the agreeable to Mrs Vansittart, whose daughter, despite all her maternal warnings, persisted in walking the poop deck on the arm of Godfrey Harland.

Mr Vansittart was also present, although he could not be numbered amongst the young people, but his genial nature made him welcome everywhere. The old gentleman was not so easy in his mind, however, as he professed to be. Sundry hints and rumours concerning Harland had greatly disturbed him lately, and he had made up his mind to speak seriously to Grace on the subject. She had refused to listen to her mother's advice, but, if necessary, he would force her to attend to his orders. He was not satisfied with what he had heard, nor with himself for having admitted a stranger so intimately to their society. However, luckily nothing was settled as yet, and he was determined to stop any further philandering until he had had an opportunity to inquire into the young man's antecedents and connections.

'Where is Grace?' were the first words he had addressed to his wife on joining her.

'I don't know, my dear,' was the reply.
'She left me half-an-hour ago—'

'Miss Vansittart is on the poop with
Mr Harland,' interposed Alice Leyton;
'I saw them walking there just now.'

'I must go and put a stop to this,'
said Mr Vansittart, commencing to button
up his greatcoat again.

His wife laid her hand on his arm.

'Not just now, my dear. Wait till
after lunch. It will look so peculiar to
drag her away from him in the sight of
everybody.'

'You are right, old lady,' he said, re-
seating himself. 'The business will keep
till after lunch.'

'What part of the country are you
going to, Alice?' demanded Miss Vere,
with a view to turning the conversation.

'We go straight home to Paradise
Farm in the Hurunni, which is about
sixty miles from Christchurch. Father
will meet us on arrival, and take us up
country. Isn't it strange? He has

never seen Winnie yet, and I do not suppose he will recognise me. I was only fourteen when I left New Zealand. How glad I shall be to see it again.'

'You love a country life, Miss Leyton ?' said Lovell.

'Oh, dearly! My father has a large sheep-run close to the Weka Pass, and we live right up in the bush, with not another house within ten miles of us. I shall milk the cows, and look after the garden and the poultry, and teach baby as much as I know myself. It is just the sort of life I love. I hate streets and towns, and a lot of houses all staring at one another.'

'And a lot of officers staring at you,' said Jack Blythe, looking in at the open door. 'Come, Alice ; be honest! You know you liked the officers at Southsea.'

'Ah! I was young then, and knew no better,' replied Alice, blushing ; 'but now I am wiser.'

'What a wonderful effect the sea air

has had upon you,' remarked Jack, laughing. 'I have heard it is considered a cure for love, but never before for vanity.'

'Oh, now, Jack, do go away!' exclaimed Alice; 'you are interrupting all our conversation.'

'Yes; and coming in just at the wrong time, and spoiling the effect of your pretty speeches. It was awfully inconsiderate of me. I will atone for it now. I will go.'

And he disappeared.

'What a bright, handsome face Mr Blythe has. I think he is one of the finest young fellows I ever saw. I wish he was in my company,' remarked Miss Vere.

'Oh, Miss Vere! I wish you would take *me* into your company, don't you know?' sighed Mr Greenwood. 'I would do anything for you, 'pon my word I would,—play parts, or take the tickets, or sweep out the theatre,—anything, only

to be near you — to see you — and feel
I was of some use, don't you know?
Couldn't you manage it, eh?'

'Why, Mr Greenwood, what do you
mean by talking of prostituting your
talents by sweeping a floor?' cried the
actress, heartily amused. 'What would
your family say to such a degradation?
No, no! What you have to do now is
to learn your part for our theatricals,
and when they are over, we'll talk about
the other thing. But we have interrupted
Alice in her description of her New Zealand home.'

'There is not much more to tell,' said
Alice. 'It is lovely, as I remember it,
and I hope I shall think it lovely still.
But—' with a long-drawn sigh—'it is the
people, and not the *place*, that make a home.'

'Just my sentiments,' replied Captain
Lovell. 'I am going to Geraldine, but
I have no friends there.'

'You will be a long way from us,' said
Alice timidly.

'Yes. But I suppose there is some sort of conveyance between the places.'

'Of course there is! You mustn't think that New Zealand is a perfectly uncivilised country. There are trains running all through it.'

'Are you going to farm, Captain Lovell?' asked Fowler.

'That is my intention. A friend of mine has bought a place out there, and I am about to join him. I know but little about ploughshares and wurzels, but my friend Cathcart is a crack hand at it all; and I am sure I shall prefer a free life to the slavery of the army. That is to say, if—if—'

'If what?' demanded Fowler.

'If I can settle down there,—make a home for myself, in fact,' said the captain, with a shy look at his inamorata.

'Persuade some one to settle down with you, you mean?' laughed his companion.

'Yes! *that* is what I mean,' acquiesced Lovell, apparently relieved to have the matter settled for him. 'What are your own plans?'

'Oh! mine are very uncertain. I may remain three months, or six, but I hope to return home *via* the Canal before a year is over my head.'

'Private business, I presume?'

'Strictly private.'

'Oh, Mr Fowler! you are so close; I am sure there is a lady in the case,' laughed Miss Vere.

'If she were anything like *you*, Miss Vere, I should pray there might be. But I have no such luck.'

'Do you know the country at all?' asked Lovell.

'I am sorry to say *no;* but I have friends out there who will soon set me all right.'

'I wonder what the shooting is like,' said the captain thoughtfully.

'Why, *I* can tell you that!' exclaimed Alice. 'The Middle Island abounds with game—Paradise ducks, grey ducks, swans, and pheasants; and if you want bigger sport, there are wild cattle and boars.'

'Is there good hunting there also?'

'Very little. We have no foxes or hares. I have seen the harriers out, but I have never known them to find.'

'That is very disappointing,' replied Lovell. 'I should have thought, since the country contains boars, there would be plenty of pig-sticking.'

'But you won't have any time for hunting. The farm will take up all your attention. You will have to plough, and reap, and harrow, and drive the cattle home. Everybody works in the bush, even the women; in fact, I think the women work almost harder than the men.'

'And why shouldn't they?' said Miss Vere. 'When women do more work in England, they will have a better claim to be acknowledged on an equality with man.'

' Do you not admit, then, that man is the superior animal, Miss Vere ? ' asked Mr Fowler, with a view to draw the actress out.

' In weight, strength, and stature, Mr Fowler—yes. But intellectually, I think his superiority is at least open to question.'

' So do I, Miss Vere,' said Dr Lennard, who had joined the party. ' I believe that the female brain only needs development, and that as civilisation advances, and *Woman* boldly asserts her rights, she will find herself absolutely equal with Man in all things.'

' But is a woman's brain as large as a man's ? ' demanded Captain Lovell, who had a head like a bullet.

' In proportion to her size there is very little difference—about one-fiftieth —which, as brain power, can easily be made up by its finer texture,' replied the doctor. ' My belief is, that the wretched education women have hitherto received has been the sole cause of their keeping in the background, and that when they obtain a fair field they will come to the front. Don't you agree with me, Miss Vere?'

'Certainly I do. See how they *have* come to the front in almost every profession they have been allowed to enter, and in so short a time too. It will not be long now before women will support themselves entirely by their own labour, and be independent of marriage and men.'

'That will be a sad day for us,' laughed Mr Fowler.

'Do you think so? I don't! I think we have sold ourselves for board and lodging long enough, and shall choose better when we are free to choose.'

'We have much to thank women for even now,' said Dr Lennard. 'The greatest geniuses the world has ever seen have repeatedly acknowledged that they owed all their moral and intellectual positions to their mothers. And it is a well-known fact, that there has never been an extraordinarily clever man born of a stupid mother, nor a giant of a little woman. And yet, in either case, the father may have been a fool or a dwarf.'

'How do you account, then, for woman's inferior position?' said Lovell.

'Because she has been kept down!' cried Miss Vere. 'She has never been allowed to enjoy the sports, or follow the vocations, to which she has an equal right with man. She has been debarred from proper exercise by a set of prudes, who consider all out-door amusements unfitted for modest and womanly women, but which are in reality the very means most necessary to develop a woman's brain, as well as her body. How then can men wonder if—if—'

'Let me assist you, Miss Vere,' interrupted the doctor. 'I think you were going to say that the corpuscles of your sex are devoid of the brain nourishing oxygen, and, if so, I quite agree with you.'

'Yes; that is what I meant, doctor; but I was too ignorant—fault of my feminine education again, you see—to find words in which to express myself.'

'Everything depends on the rearing of girls,' remarked Dr Lennard. 'Parents are careful to bring up their sons to healthful occupations and exercises, but their daughters are but too often doomed, by the injustice and short-sighted folly of the world, to a life of inertion.'

'Hardly *injustice*, doctor,' said Mrs Vansittart; 'it is their own choice. I am sure women have every liberty now-a-days.'

'Yes, *injustice*. The doctor is perfectly right. There is no other word for it,' exclaimed Alice, suddenly bursting into eloquence.

'So you are going to take up the gauntlet for your sex?' laughed the doctor. 'You do not look a very ill-used person, though, Miss Alice, with that rose-leaf complexion and peachy cheek.'

' Doctor, it is very rude to be so personal. You quite confuse me. What was I talking about?' said the girl.

' Injustice to your lovely sex,' replied Mr Fowler.

' Oh, yes. Why have many of our cleverest women written under an assumed name, and signed their works by a masculine one, except that they knew how difficult it is to convince the world that anything really good can be produced by a woman. And then you deny that men are unjust to us.'

' Why, Alice, you astonish me. I had no idea that you could talk so well,' said Captain Lovell, as she finished her peroration.

But if her eloquence had astonished the young officer, his familiarity with her surprised his hearers still more. It was the first time he had called her by her Christian name in public, and Alice coloured scarlet as she heard it.   A painful pause ensued, in which Miss Vere came to the rescue.

'Well, it seems to me,' she said, 'that in discussing women's brains, we have quite forgotten that we met to discuss the private theatricals.   Miss Leyton, have you quite decided to play "Julia" to Captain Lovell's "Faulkner"?'

'Yes, quite, I think,' replied Alice, who was still as red as a peony.

'Then we must fix on the dresses.   I think you told me you had a white dress that—'

'There is such a splendid ship in sight, do you know?' exclaimed Harold Green- wood, suddenly bursting in upon them. 'She has four masts, and is going to Calcutta.   Won't you come on deck and see her, eh?'

'Oh, we must run up and see the ship,' cried everybody, as they deserted the smoke-room.

CHAPTER XIV.

SETTLED.

THE large vessel, which turned out to be the *Carrickfergus*, of Glasgow, bound for Calcutta, did not appear to interest Alice Leyton and Captain Lovell. They gazed at her for a few moments in silence, and then turned away, as if by mutual consent, and walked to the other side of the deck together.

'Why don't you stay and watch them pulling up the flags?' said Alice, as she perceived that the captain had followed her.

'Because I would far rather be with you. Alice, what is the matter? What have I done to offend you?'

'Do I look offended?'

'You do not smile as sweetly as usual, and I am miserable. Is it possible you are angry with me?'

'Yes, I am—a little. Why did you call me "Alice" before all those people? You know you have no right to do so, and the next thing we shall hear, is that it is reported all over the ship we are engaged.'

'Then let us forestall their gossip, and make the report true. Let us be engaged, Alice.'

'How can we, when mother won't hear of it? She says everything must remain *in statu quo* until she sees my father. I believe she is half sorry I have broken with Jack Blythe. She is always extolling his bravery and courage to the skies, because he jumped in the sea after baby. I wish,' continued Alice, with a suspicious moisture in her blue eyes, 'I do wish, Robert, that *you* had been the one to save her. Then mother would have thought nothing too good for *you.*'

'Oh, my darling! don't you believe I *would* have done so if Blythe had not forestalled me? I was looking after *you*, you know ; and it would have been of no use *two* of us jumping into the water at the same time—would it, now?'

'No, I suppose not,' replied Alice, with a sigh ; 'but baby is all the world to mother.'

'Then she will have the less trouble in making up her mind to part with you, Alice! I have been half afraid to speak openly to you since that interview with Mrs Leyton. She seemed so dead set against my suit. But I think we ought to understand each other. The matter really concerns only you and me, and I want to have something definite to say to your father when I meet him. Tell me the truth, then. Do you love me?'

'Oh, Robert! I think you *know* I do,' whispered Alice.

'Better than you loved Mr Blythe?'

'I don't think now that I ever really loved him. I *liked* him very much. He is a dear, good fellow. I like him still, but I feel I could never *marry* him.'

'And could you marry *me*, darling?'

Alice's blushes spoke for her. She was not much more than a child in years, but her womanhood was born at that moment, and she felt her heart leaping in mighty throbs to welcome it. But her tongue refused to utter the thoughts that were surging in her brain.

'Can't you speak to me?' pleaded Captain Lovell presently. 'Just say, "Robert, I love you, and I will be your wife," and my heart will be at rest for ever more.'

Alice turned her big blue eyes suddenly upon him.

'I love you,' she said rapidly, 'and I will be your wife.'

And then, as if frightened at the sound of her own boldness, she flushed scarlet from brow to bosom, and the tears rushed to her eyes. Lovell thought he had never seen her look so pretty as when she stood thus, burning with love and shame, before him.

' My darling!' he exclaimed, 'how I wish that I could kiss you! But a hundred eyes are on us, and I can only thank you for your consent by word of mouth. Thank you a thousand times, my wife that is to be! I shall be as brave as a lion, Alice, with your sweet promise to urge me on. And now, let the people say what they choose. We *are* engaged to one another, and no one can part us, unless your father does. So let us be as happy as we can till we reach New Zealand, and not anticipate an evil that may never come.'

' Here are Miss Vere and Mr Fowler. Talk of something else,' said Alice, in a fearful whisper.

'Tell me how you employ yourself all day long at Paradise Farm, Miss Leyton,' replied Lovell, taking the cue.

'Oh, there are no end of things to be done! The day is not half long enough I help mother in the house during the mornings, and in the afternoons I ride or drive or garden, according to the weather.'

'Or pay horrid social calls,' suggested the captain.

'Not often—that is, in up-country stations. The distances are too great. The nearest dwelling-house to ours is ten miles off. But we drive to the town sometimes, and to afternoon dances and teas.'

'And in the evenings?'

'We read books or do crewel work, and go to bed at ten.'

'Whew!' said Lovell, giving a long, low whistle; 'what an awful existence!'

'Don't try it, then,' returned Alice archly; 'for everybody does the same.

We rise at four or five, have dinner at one (and it usually consists of mutton in every shape and form), tea at six, and all lights out at ten. You will soon fall into the custom, and begin yawning at nine o'clock.'

'But what work can such little hands as yours do ?'

'Everything! There are very few servants in New Zealand, and the squatters' wives and daughters do all the cooking, washing, and cleaning themselves. Sometimes I saddle father's horse or my own, and if he is busy, I chop up wood for the fire, and draw the water for the use of the house.'

'I cannot believe it. You are joking with me! Such work is not fit for such a delicate creature as you are,' said Lovell, looking genuinely distressed.

'Indeed, I am not delicate; and if I were, I would help my parents all in my power. I shall always work for them whilst I am at home.'

'I hope you will not be at home long, my darling,' whispered her lover.

'If not, I shall work in the house I go to,' whispered Alice, in return.

'Not while I have a hand to do it for you,' said Lovell. 'Alice! if you will consent to come and brighten my poor home with the sunshine of your presence, you must promise to leave the hard work to some one else.'

'I will promise to do exactly as you tell me, Robert,' she answered; 'but I'm afraid we are attracting attention, and it must be nearly time for luncheon. Here comes Mr and Miss Vansittart. Let me go back to mother! I feel as if everybody must guess what we have been talking of, from my face.'

'Little goose—' said Lovell fondly, as he handed her down the companion.

Mr Vansittart was talking so seriously to his daughter, that they had not even noticed the presence of the lovers.

'Gracie, my dear,' he had commenced

by saying, 'I wants to have a little
chat with you about Mr Harland. You
two seem to be taking up with one another, to my mind, and so I think it
right to warn you before it goes too
far.'

'To *warn* me, papa?' said Grace,
with open eyes. 'Of *what?*'

'Why, that before any gentleman pro-
poses to be your husband, he must be
prepared to satisfy me concerning his
family, and his character, and his means
of making a living. And I am afraid
Mr Harland is *not* prepared to do so.'

'Why should you say that, papa? I
think it is bitterly unfair.'

'No, my dear! there ain't no fairness
nor unfairness about it. It's just a
matter of business. I'm sorry to see
as Mr Harland is not a favourite aboard
ship, and there's one or two nasty tales
floating about concerning his card-play-
ing that have quite choked me off him.
And so I consider it's time I looked a

bit after the way he's going on with you. You see, my dear, I don't know anything about the young man's antecedents.'

'Then I wonder at your bringing him out to Tabbakooloo with us, papa.'

'Well, that was my mistake, Grace. But then I brought him out as a land-agent, remember, and not as a son-in-law! I can dismiss the one, but there's no dismissing of the other. And so it behoves us to be careful. Now tell me candidly how far you've got with him.'

'I don't understand you, papa,' said Miss Grace, who, when offended, often professed not to be able to comprehend her parents' meaning.

'D—n it all, then, I'll put it plainer,' said Mr Vansittart, getting angry. 'How much sweethearting's gone on between you? Has he spoken to you of marriage?'

'Sometimes ; naturally!'

'Has he asked you downright to marry him ?'

' He has intimated that he wished it.'

' And what did you say ? '

' Nothing, papa—'

' You're not engaged to him, nor any rubbish of that sort, then ? '

' Oh, no ! How could I be, without asking your consent, and mamma's ? But Godfrey—I mean Mr Harland—has told me several times that he only waits till we arrive at Tabbakooloo to make formal proposals for my hand.'

' Formal fiddlesticks ! If he was half a man, he'd have spoken up at once. I'm very much afraid it ain't all right. And so, look here, my girl, whatever Harland may do when he gets ashore, remember it's my orders as nothing more goes on between you now. When he speaks to me, he'll get my answer ; but I won't have any more sweethearting aboard this ship ; and if you disobey me, I shall take means to keep you apart.'

' But, papa, I can't be cool to Mr Harland. Every one knows he is your agent.'

'I don't want you to be cool to him, but I won't have any love-making. Your mother saw him kiss you last night in the cabin passage. You must put a stop to that sort of thing at once. Do you fully understand me?'

'Fully,' replied Miss Vansittart, who fully understood her own intentions also.

'I don't believe the fellow's got a sixpence to jingle on a tombstone,' continued Mr Vansittart, waxing warmer at his daughter's reticence; 'and a pauper don't marry my only child. It's like his impudence to dream of it. Not that I would have made his poverty an objection (having so much myself), if it hadn't been for those other things. But a man as cheats at play, must be bad all round.'

'Who *dares* to say that he cheats at play?' exclaimed Grace Vansittart, firing up in defence of her absent lover. 'It's a lie, father. I am sure of it. Mr Harland would be incapable of such a meanness.'

'Well, I hope so, my dear, but I must know a little more about it before I decide. Besides, that's not all. He had a violent quarrel with some low fellow in the second cabin the other night, and part of their conversation was overheard, and has got about the ship, and it isn't nice—not nice at all. So, you see, until I can be satisfied of the falseness of such rumours, I can't do less than warn you, my dear, not to show anything more than civility to Mr Harland. If I find on further inquiry that they are true, I shall give him his return passage-money, and his dismissal, as soon as ever we touch land, for I won't have such a man at Tabbakooloo.'

Grace was weeping silently by this time beneath her veil. She was a proud, self-willed girl, and she would let her father see neither her tears nor her determination to have her own way. But she foresaw the trouble and opposition that would ensue, and felt much injured in consequence.

'You don't answer me,' continued Mr Vansittart, perceiving she was sulky, 'and I daresay you feel a bit disappointed; but I mean what I say, and I intend you shall obey me. And don't forget I shall be keeping a sharp eye on you, my girl, so it's no use trying to deceive me. And now go down to your lunch, and don't let's hear any more of the subject.'

Grace dried her tears, and obeyed her father's behest, but she felt obstinately rebellious the while. Matters had gone much further between her and Godfrey Harland than her parents had any idea of, but they would never learn the truth now from her. She was one of those women—very few and far between—who have the power to keep their own secrets. The day came, and not so long after, when Grace Vansittart was forced to acknowledge the justice of her father's commands, but she never gave him the satisfaction of hearing so. The day dawned also when the weeks she spent on board the *Pandora* were things of the past, and a new life had opened before her — a life in which ' Charlie Monro ' took a part, and Mrs Vansittart's prayers for her daughter's future were fulfilled.

But had Charlie been fully acquainted with all that had transpired during the voyage to New Zealand, would Grace Vansittart ever have been transformed into Mrs Monro? Who can tell? If all our inmost secrets were laid bare, would any one of us, male or female, occupy the positions which we hold in the estimation of the world?

The most exciting part of transmigration to another sphere, must surely be the fact that in that ærial ' Palace of Truth ' we are promised the secrets of all hearts shall be revealed.

CHAPTER XV.

THE LETTER.

T may be remembered that a certain letter written by Mr Vansittart to Godfrey Harland, and left by that gentleman in his coat pocket, was the means by which Iris discovered his intention to desert her. Strange to say, Harland had never missed the letter. He only visited his home on one occasion after that evening, and then the excitement of his new prospects, and the necessity of keeping up appearances to deceive his wife, had prevented his discovering his loss. Iris had preserved the paper carefully, and brought it with her on board the *Pandora*. She intended to produce it in proof of her right to have followed her husband to New Zealand ; and, in case of his attempting to excuse himself, to confront him with the witness to his treachery. When Maggie told her that Godfrey was paying open court to Grace Vansittart, Iris took out her box of letters, and turned them over, and read that one amongst others, to see if she could discover that he had had any positive intention of committing bigamy before he started on the voyage,—whether, in fact, his wooing of Miss Vansittart was the result of an unfortunate passion, or of a premeditated crime. And, in putting back her papers, she dropped Mr Vansittart's note upon the cabin floor. It was picked up and read by Will Farrell. As he was debating what to do with it—having pro-mised Maggie Greet that he would never divulge to Iris that he knew her to be Godfrey Harland's wife—Iris herself came into the cabin, and walked its length with her eyes upon the floor, as though searching for something.

'Have you lost anything, Miss Douglas?' asked Farrell, as he watched her.

'Yes, I have dropped a letter—a very important letter. Have you seen it, steward?' she said, in her sweet, low voice.

'No, miss, I ain't,' replied the steward. 'When did you have it last?'

'Only this morning. I was reading over some old letters, and this one amongst them. It is written on thick, glazed paper, and has a large monogram in red and gold at the top. I shall be very vexed if I lose it.'

'Well, I'll find it for you if it's aboard, miss. But p'r'aps it's blowed over. The wind has been very fresh through the cabin, to-day,' replied the steward, jingling his glasses.

'Oh! I *hope* not!' exclaimed Iris, clasp-

ing her hands in genuine distress. 'It
is of the utmost consequence to me. Pray
look for it at once, steward ; it may have
got into your pantry, amongst the breakfast things.'

The steward bundled off into his sanc-
tum, and Will Farrell approached her
with the letter in his hand.

'Is this what you are looking for, Miss
Douglas ? '

Iris flushed scarlet.

'Oh, yes, it is indeed ! I am so much
obliged to you ! Where did you find it ? '

'Under the table. I picked it up about
an hour ago.'

Iris took the letter, and twisted it about
nervously in her fingers.

'Mr Farrell, have you read it ? ' she said
at last timidly.

'Yes, Miss Douglas, I have, and, beg-
ging your pardon, I should like to know
how it came into your possession.'

He knew well enough, but he said it
to force her to a confession of the truth.

'I—I don't quite understand you,' she stammered.

'I mean how is it that you hold a letter addressed to Godfrey Harland ?'

'Do you know him ?' she asked quickly.

'*Know him !* I should rather think I did. I know him for the greatest scoundrel unhung.'

'Hush !—hush !' cried Iris fearfully.

'I'm not afraid of who may hear me, Miss Douglas. The whole ship might listen, for ought I should care about it. But I am sorry to think so true a lady as yourself should have any connection (however distant) with such a blackguard as Godfrey Harland.'

'Ah! you don't know—' she commenced, with a look of the keenest pain.

'Won't you tell me ?' he said coaxingly. 'I'm a rough fellow, Miss Douglas, and not a fit friend, perhaps, for the like of you. But I can see you're in trouble, and if your trouble is connected with that man, you'll want a friend to help you through with it. He's a rascal—I can't help saying it, whatever you may think of him, and if he can cheat you, he will, as he has done others, over and over again.'

' Oh! I think I could trust you!' exclaimed Iris involuntarily; 'for you look honest and true, Mr Farrell, and you love Maggie, and Maggie loves me. Yes, I feel sure you will be the friend of *her* friend. But how astonished you will be when I tell you the truth! Stoop your head lower, that no one may hear us. My name is not Miss Douglas at all. It is Iris Harland. I am Godfrey Harland's wife.'

' God help you, poor thing!' exclaimed Farrell fervently.

' Ah! what do you know against him to say that ?' she replied, shrinking from him. ' Did you ever hear of him before you met on board ship ?'

' I have known him, to my misfortune, for years, Miss Douglas. He has been the ruin of my life.'

'God forgive him!   How?'

'We were clerks in the same office, though he was in a higher position than myself, and his real name (as I suppose you know) is Horace Cain.'

'*Horace Cain!*' repeated Iris, with knitted brows.   'I never heard of it.   Mr Farrell, are you *sure* you are not making a mistake?   He married me as Godfrey Harland.'

'Then he married you under a false name.   But he had good reason for changing it, as I will prove to you.   How well I remember the day his father, old Mr Cain, brought him to Starling's office, and what a swell we all thought him!   He had only left college a few weeks then, owing to their loss of fortune, and he gave himself all the airs of a millionaire.   We were very much prejudiced against him at first, because old Starling (who was a friend of his father's) placed him over all our heads, although he did not know anything of the business.   However, it was his policy to make himself agreeable, and learn all he could. And nice work he made of the knowledge he gained. He hadn't been six months in the office, before a forgery was committed on old Starling's bank for eight hundred pounds.

' Mr Farrell,' cried Iris, turning very white, as she clutched his arm, ' it was not *Godfrey* who did it ? '

' It certainly was, Miss Douglas.'

'Oh, no, no! He is very bad. He is cruel and false and ungenerous, I know, but *surely* he never committed such an awful crime.'

' Miss Douglas, Harland was the forger of that cheque, as sure as we sit here. He has never denied it to me. He *cannot*. There were but two of us who *could* have done it—he and myself—and *I* know that it was not I.

' But how could he escape ? '

' He bolted to America, leaving a very cleverly-concocted letter behind him to say that he knew that the suspicion would falsely fall upon himself, and that he was unable either to bear such a calumny, or turn Queen's evidence against one whom he had treated as a friend. And by the time the letter was received, he was clear off under an assumed name, having left part of the receipts for the forged cheque (which he sent *me* to cash) in my desk, where, to my utter amazement, they were found, rolled up in some old bills. Suspicion, of course, fell upon me, but Cain's conduct in running away was so mysterious, that we were considered to be partners in crime, and as Mr Starling, for his old friend's sake, would institute no proceedings against Horace, he refused also to prosecute me. But he turned me out of his office without a character, and a stain upon my name, and the curse has followed me ever since. I have tried again and again, Miss Douglas, to procure permanent employment. I have even stooped to menial service, with the same result. I get on well; I grow in favour with my employers ; I work hard—and then, just as I am rising to something better, the curse comes down upon me, the old lie crops up. I am dubbed as a suspected *forger*, and dismissed without ceremony. It is this that sickened me of trying to live in England, and determined me to try my fortune in another land. In New Zealand the old story may be forgotten, and, if not, I shall find others as bad as myself. And now you know, Miss Douglas, why I *hate* Godfrey Harland. I met him before we started, and warned him not to come near me during the voyage. He has chosen to disregard that warning, and we have had a quarrel over it. If he does it a second time, I have threatened to expose him to the whole ship's company, and I will keep my word. I will yet pay Horace Cain out for the cruel turn he did me years ago.'

'Oh, Mr Farrell, don't say that !' exclaimed Iris, who had grown as white as a sheet as she listened to the disgraceful story. 'Hard as it is for me to say it, remember he is my husband, and I am bound to live with him. For God's sake don't make my position worse than it need be. I can't tell you how I dread the prospect now. But as the wife of *a forger!* Oh, heavens! it is too much, even for *me* to bear!'

And she drooped her head upon the table and buried her face in her hands.

'*Too much*,' repeated Farrell. 'I should think it *was* too much. It is sacrilege to think of such a thing. Miss Douglas, you must not go back to him. He is not worthy of a second thought from you. By your own confession, he has made you miserable—else why are you following him under an assumed name, instead of openly proclaiming yourself his wife?'

'I was afraid,' faltered Iris. 'He deserted me,—left me to starve and—'

'And took to courting Miss Vansittart instead. Cannot you see the little game

he is playing now, Miss Douglas. He
wants to add bigamy to his other mis-
demeanours. He has an idea of marrying
his employer's daughter, and getting a
handsome dowry with her, I suppose. I
know he has given himself out as an un-
married man, and all the ship imagines
they are an engaged couple.'

'Maggie has told me the same,' cried
Iris excitedly, 'but I cannot believe it.
How could he be so foolish, when he knows
that I live, and any mail might take out a
letter to reveal the truth. Besides, notwithstanding all his unkindness to me, I
did think sometimes that he loved me a
little.

'There speaks your woman's vanity,
Miss Douglas, and not your common
sense. How can any man *love* the
woman whom he makes miserable. But
if you doubt his motives respecting Miss
Vansittart, watch them, and judge for
yourself.'

'How can I watch them from this

cabin.   I only see them sometimes in the evenings walking together on the poop.'

'They have theatricals to-night, you know, in the little theatre that the sailors rigged up in the after-part of the vessel. Go and see them, and you will probably have a domestic drama enacted for your private benefit.   Both Mr Harland and Miss Vansittart have refused to act. They prefer sitting together in the semi-darkness in front.   Take my advice, and when you come back to this cabin, you will tell me your mind is made up.'

'But if I should be seen ?   I have been so very careful since coming on board, to keep out of his way.'

'But *why ?*   What is your object in concealing yourself, now that we are out at sea ?'

'I don't quite know,' faltered Iris ; 'but I am so afraid of him.   He is so violent, you know, when he is disturbed.'

'And will he be less so on land ?   Or

do you think you will have more protection from him there than here ? Miss
Douglas, excuse me for saying I think
you are quite wrong. As you *have* followed him (which seems to have been a
great mistake to me), the sooner you discover yourself the better. Every day
you keep the truth from him you increase
the chance of Miss Vansittart being made
as unhappy as yourself. I don't know
what sort of a girl she is, but since *you*
could be deceived by his false tongue
into believing him to be good and true,
I suppose she may be the same.'

' Oh, how I wish I had never followed
him !' exclaimed Iris ; 'but what was I to
do ? He left us (Maggie and me) without money or credit or anything, just to
steal or starve as we thought fit. And
I was indignant with him, and I knew it
was his duty to support me, and so I decided to come too. And now I feel as if
I would rather drown than go through
what lies before me.'

'Don't think of yourself. Think of Miss Vansittart,' urged Farrell. 'It is bitterly unfair that she should be a victim as well as you.'

'Yes, I *will* think of her, poor girl,' said Iris, 'and if I am convinced that Godfrey means harm to her—'

'Watch them when they think they are unobserved, and you will soon be convinced of it, Miss Douglas. The sailors could tell you some fine stories of their sweethearting on deck after dark. The girl is infatuated with him. And I think his only object is to get her so completely in his power that she shall marry him on landing, whether her parents consented to it or not.'

'It shall never go as far as that,' said Iris, clenching her teeth.

'Then prevent it going any further now, for the sake of your own dignity, and that of your sex, Miss Douglas. You may think you know Mr Harland's character thoroughly, but I am sure you are not aware of half of what he is capable. Let me take you to the performance this evening, and I will guarantee you shall not be discovered. You can pretend you have the faceache, and wrap your head up in a veil, and I will place you in a dark corner where you shall see without being seen.'

'Yes! I *will* go,' replied Iris determinedly. 'Even if the price were to be instantaneous discovery, I would go.'

'And if you find the case to be as I have described it to you?'

'If I have self-evident proofs that my husband is deceiving this girl by making love to her, I will go to him at once, and tell him I have discovered his plans, and will circumvent them.

'Bravo! Miss Douglas. That is spoken like a brave woman. I was certain you would eventually decide *that* to be the only honest course before you. But why are you crying? Surely you do not consider Godfrey Harland to be worthy of your tears?'

'Oh, Mr Farrell! you do not understand,' sobbed Iris. 'You do not know how hard it is for a woman to come to the conclusion that she has been wasting all her love on an unworthy object. I am not weeping for the loss of *him*. I am weeping for the loss of my self-respect,—of my faith in my fellow-creatures,—my faith in my own judgment and discrimination. I feel so crushed —so humiliated—so ashamed, and as if I never could put trust in anything on earth again.'

'Well! I don't know as it's wise to do it at any time,' replied Farrell; 'but "one swallow doesn't make a summer." You should take pattern by Maggie. She seems to have had a rough time of it, poor child, but she's willing to throw it all behind her back, and try again.'

'*Has* Maggie been unhappy?' in-

quired Iris, drying her eyes. She
never told me so. And yet sometimes I
have fancied there was *something* which
she kept to herself, when she has been
particularly kind and loving to me. Oh!
she is a dear good girl, Mr Farrell, and I
am sure she will repay your love to her.
I cannot tell you what she has been to
me all through my wretched married life.'

'Well, the ways of women are queer,'
said Farrell, scratching his head thoughtfully, 'and I don't pretend to understand
them. But I'm sure of one thing, that
whatever Maggie is, or has been, she
loves you, Miss Douglas, just like her
own life. And she'd give up her life for
yours any day into the bargain. I'm as
sure of it as I am that there's a heaven
above us.'

'And so am I,' responded Iris warmly,
as she made her escape to her own cabin.

END OF VOL. II.